D0456461

CENTRAL LINE

'Reading these tales is like listening to someone talking: someone – in this most simply pleasurable collection of all – you very much want to hear'

Sunday Telegraph

'Maeve Binchy reads the fantasies and lives of others with devastating clarity. Her distinction is that her stories are dramatically credible'

Scotsman

'Each story is an absolute delight . . . All have a perceptive warmth and love of humanity . . . Maeve Binchy's story-telling art is exquisite. It is immensely readable'

East Anglian Daily Times

Maeve Binchy was born in Dublin, and went to school at the Holy Child Convent in Killiney. She took a history degree at UCD and taught in various girls' schools, writing travel articles in the long summer holidays. In 1969 she joined the *Irish Times*. For the last eight years she has been based in London and writes humorous columns from all over the world. The Peacock Theatre in Dublin was the scene of her two stage plays, *End of Term* and *Half Promised Land*, and her television play, *Deeply Regretted By*, won two Jacobs Awards and the Best Script Award at the Prague Film Festival. She is the author of two other volumes of short stories, *Victoria Line* and *Dublin 4* and of the bestselling novel, *Light A Penny Candle*. Maeve Binchy is married to the writer and broadcaster Gordon Snell.

Central Line

Maeve Binchy

CORONET BOOKS
Hodder and Stoughton

To Gordon with all my love

Copyright © 1978, 1979, 1980, 1982 by Maeve Binchy

Central Line was first published in Great Britain in 1983 by Quartet Books and Ward River Press Limited. It appeared as part of a hardback edition entitled *London Transports* published by Century Ltd in 1983.

Coronet edition 1984.
British Library C.I.P.

Binchy, Maeve
  Central Line
  I. Title
  823'.914[F]   PR6052.17728

ISBN 0–340–33992–6

The characters and situations in this book are entirely imaginary and bear no relation to any real person or actual happening.

This book is sold subject to the condition that it shall not, by way of trade or otherwise, be lent, re-sold, hired out or otherwise circulated without the publisher's prior consent in any form of binding or cover other than that in which this is published and without a similar condition including this condition being imposed on the subsequent purchaser.

Printed and bound in Great Britain for Hodder and Stoughton Paperbacks, a division of Hodder and Stoughton Ltd., Mill Road, Dunton Green, Sevenoaks, Kent (Editorial Office: 47 Bedford Square, London, WC1 3DP) by Cox & Wyman Ltd., Reading

Contents

Shepherd's Bush

People looked very weary, May thought, and shabbier than she had remembered Londoners to be. They reminded her a little of those news-reel pictures of crowds during the war or just after it, old raincoats, brave smiles, endless patience. But then this wasn't Regent Street where she had wandered up and down looking at shops on other visits to London, it wasn't the West End with lights all glittering and people getting out of taxis full of excitement and wafts of perfume. This was Shepherd's Bush where people lived. They had probably set out from here early this morning and fought similar crowds on the way to work. The women must have done their shopping in their lunch-hour because most of them were carrying plastic bags of food. It was a London different to the one you see as a tourist.

And she was here for a different reason, although she had once read a cynical article in a magazine which said that girls coming to London for abortions provided a significant part of the city's tourist revenue. It wasn't something you could classify under any terms as a holiday. When she filled in the card at the airport she had written 'Business' in the section where it said 'Purpose of journey'.

The pub where she was to meet Celia was near the tube station. She found it easily and settled herself in. A lot of the accents were Irish, workmen having a pint before they went home to their English wives and their television programmes. Not drunk tonight, it was only Monday, but obviously regulars. Maybe not so welcome as regulars on Friday or Saturday nights, when they would remember they were Irish and sing anti-British songs.

Celia wouldn't agree with her about that. Celia had rose-tinted views about the Irish in London, she thought they were all here from choice, not because there was no work for them at home. She hated stories about the restless Irish, or Irishmen on the lump in the building trade. She said people shouldn't make such a big thing about it all. People who came from much farther away settled in London, it was big enough to absorb everyone. Oh well, she wouldn't bring up the subject, there were enough things to disagree with Celia about . . . without searching for more.

Oh why of all people, of all the bloody people in the world, did she have to come to Celia? Why was there nobody else whom she could ask for advice? Celia would give it, she would give a lecture with every piece of information she imparted. She would deliver a speech with every cup of tea, she would be cool, practical and exactly the right person, if she weren't so much the wrong person. It was handing Celia a whole box of ammunition about Andy. From now on Celia could say that Andy was a rat, and May could no longer say she had no facts to go on.

Celia arrived. She was thinner, and looked a little tired. She smiled. Obviously the lectures weren't going to come in the pub. Celia always knew the right place for things. Pubs were for meaningless chats and bright, non-intense conversation. Home was for lectures.

'You're looking marvellous,' Celia said.

It couldn't be true. May looked at her reflection in a glass panel. You couldn't see the dark lines under her eyes there, but you could see the droop of her shoulders, she wasn't a person that could be described as looking marvellous. No, not even in a pub.

'I'm okay,' she said. 'But you've got very slim, how did you do it?'

'No bread, no cakes, no potatoes, no sweets,' said Celia in a business-like way. 'It's the old rule but it's the only rule. You deny yourself everything you want and you lose weight.'

'I know,' said May, absently rubbing her waistline.

'Oh I didn't mean *that*,' cried Celia horrified. 'I didn't mean that at all.'

May felt weary, she hadn't meant that either, she was patting her stomach because she had been putting on weight. The child that she was going to get rid of was still only a speck, it would cause no bulge. She had put on weight because she cooked for Andy three or four times a week in his flat. He was long and lean. He could eat for ever and he wouldn't put on weight. He didn't like eating alone so she ate with him. She reassured Celia that there was no offence and when Celia had gone, twittering with rage at herself, to the counter, May wondered whether she had explored every avenue before coming to Celia and Shepherd's Bush for help.

She had. There were no legal abortions in Dublin, and she did not know of anyone who had ever had an illegal one there. England and the ease of the system were less than an hour away by plane. She didn't want to try and get it on the National Health, she had the money, all she wanted was someone who would introduce her to a doctor, so that she could get it all over with quickly. She needed somebody who knew her, somebody who wouldn't abandon her if things went wrong, somebody who would lie for her, because a few lies would have to be told. May didn't have any other friends in London. There was a girl she had once met on a skiing holiday, but you couldn't impose on a holiday friendship in that way. She knew a man, a very nice, kind man who had stayed in the hotel where she worked and had often begged her to come and stay with him and his wife. But she couldn't go to stay with them for the first time in this predicament, it would be ridiculous. It had to be Celia.

It might be easier if Celia had loved somebody so much that everything else was unimportant. But stop, that wasn't fair. Celia loved that dreary, boring, selfish Martin. She loved him so much that she believed one day he was going to get things organized and make a home for them. Everyone else knew that Martin was the worst possible bet for any punter, a Mamma's boy, who had everything he wanted now, including a visit every two months from Celia, home from London, smartly-dressed, undemanding, saving away for a day that would never come. So Celia did under-

9

stand something about the nature of love. She never talked about it. People as brisk as Celia don't talk about things like unbrisk attitudes in men, or hurt feelings or broken hearts. Not when it refers to themselves, but they are very good at pointing out the foolish attitudes of others.

Celia was back with the drinks.

'We'll finish them up quickly,' she said.

Why could she never, never take her ease over anything? Things always had to be finished up quickly. It was warm and anonymous in the pub. They could go back to Celia's flat, which May felt sure wouldn't have even a comfortable chair in it, and talk in a business-like way about the rights and wrongs of abortion, the procedure, the money, and how it shouldn't be spent on something so hopeless and destructive. And about Andy. Why wouldn't May tell him? He had a right to know. The child was half his, and even if he didn't want it he should pay for the abortion. He had plenty of money, he was a hotel manager. May had hardly any, she was a hotel receptionist. May could see it all coming, she dreaded it. She wanted to stay in this warm place until closing-time, and to fall asleep, and wake up there two days later.

Celia made walking-along-the-road conversation on the way to her flat. This road used to be very quiet and full of retired people, now it was all flats and bed-sitters. That road was nice, but noisy, too much through-traffic. The houses in the road over there were going for thirty-five thousand, which was ridiculous, but then you had to remember it was fairly central and they did have little gardens. Finally they were there. A big Victorian house, a clean, polished hall, and three flights of stairs. The flat was much bigger than May expected, and it had a sort of divan on which she sat down immediately and put up her legs, while Celia fussed about a bit, opening a bottle of wine and putting a dish of four small lamb chops into the oven. May braced herself for the lecture.

It wasn't a lecture, it was an information-sheet. She was so relieved that she could feel herself relaxing, and filled up her wineglass again.

'I've arranged with Doctor Harris that you can call to see him tomorrow morning at 11. I told him no lies, just a little less than the truth. I said you were staying with me.

If he thinks that means you are staying permanently, that's his mistake not mine. I mentioned that your problem was . . . what it is. I asked him when he thought it would be . . . em . . . done. He said Wednesday or Thursday, but it would all depend. He didn't seem shocked or anything; it's like tonsillitis to him, I suppose. Anyway he was very calm about it. I think you'll find he's a kind person and it won't be upsetting . . . that part of it.'

May was dumbfounded. Where were the accusations, the I-told-you-so sighs, the hope that now, finally, she would finish with Andy? Where was the slight moralistic bit, the heavy wondering whether or not it might be murder? For the first time in the eleven days since she had confirmed she was pregnant, May began to hope that there would be some normality in the world again.

'Will it embarrass you, all this?' she asked. 'I mean, do you feel it will change your relationship with him?'

'In London a doctor isn't an old family friend like at home, May. He's someone you go to, or I've gone to anyway, when I've had to have my ears syringed, needed antibiotics for flu last year, and a medical certificate for the time I sprained my ankle and couldn't go to work. He hardly knows me except as a name on his register. He's nice though, and he doesn't rush you in and out. He's Jewish and small and worried-looking.'

Celia moved around the flat, changing into comfortable sitting-about clothes, looking up what was on television, explaining to May that she must sleep in her room and that she, Celia, would use the divan.

No, honestly, it would be easier that way, she wasn't being nice, it would be much easier. A girl friend rang and they arranged to play squash together at the week-end. A wrong number rang; a West Indian from the flat downstairs knocked on the door to say he would be having a party on Saturday night and to apologize in advance for any noise. If they liked to bring a bottle of something, they could call in themselves. Celia served dinner. They looked at television for an hour, then went to bed.

May thought what a strange empty life Celia led here far from home, miles from Martin, no real friends, no life at all. Then she thought that Celia might possibly regard her life too as sad, working in a second-rate hotel for five

11

years, having an affair with its manager for three years. A hopeless affair because the manager's wife and four children were a bigger stumbling-block than Martin's mother could ever be. She felt tired and comfortable, and in Celia's funny, characterless bedroom she drifted off and dreamed that Andy had discovered where she was and what she was about to do, and had flown over during the night to tell her that they would get married next morning, and live in England and forget the hotel, the family and what anyone would say.

Tuesday morning. Celia was gone. Dr Harris's address was neatly written on the pad by the phone with instructions how to get there. Also Celia's phone number at work, and a message that May never believed she would hear from Celia. 'Good luck.'

He was small, and Jewish, and worried and kind. His examination was painless and unembarrassing. He confirmed what she knew already. He wrote down dates, and asked general questions about her health. May wondered whether he had a family, there were no pictures of wife or children in the surgery. But then there were none in Andy's office, either. Perhaps his wife was called Rebecca and she too worried because her husband worked so hard, they might have two children, a boy who was a gifted musician, and a girl who wanted to get married to a Christian. Maybe they all walked along these leafy roads on Saturdays to synagogue and Rebecca cooked all those things like gefilte fish and bagels.

With a start, May told herself to stop dreaming about him. It was a habit she had got into recently, fancying lives for everyone she met, however briefly. She usually gave them happy lives with a bit of problem-to-be-solved thrown in. She wondered what a psychiatrist would make of that. As she was coming back to real life, Dr Harris was saying that if he was going to refer her for a termination he must know why she could not have the baby. He pointed out that she was healthy, and strong, and young. She should have no difficulty with pregnancy or birth. Were there emotional reasons? Yes, it would kill her parents, she wouldn't be able to look after the baby, she didn't want to look after one on her own either, it wouldn't be fair on her or the baby.

12

'And the father?' Dr Harris asked.

'Is my boss, is heavily married, already has four babies of his own. It would break up his marriage which he doesn't want to do ... yet. No, the father wouldn't want me to have it either.'

'Has he said that?' asked Dr Harris as if he already knew the answer.

'I haven't told him, I can't tell him, I won't tell him,' said May.

Dr Harris sighed. He asked a few more questions; he made a telephone call; he wrote out an address. It was a posh address near Harley Street.

'This is Mr White. A well-known surgeon. These are his consulting-rooms, I have made an appointment for you at 2.30 this afternoon. I understand from your friend Miss ...' He searched his mind and his desk for Celia's name and then gave up. 'I understand anyway that you are not living here, and don't want to try and pretend that you are, so that you want the termination done privately. That's just as well, because it would be difficult to get it done on the National Health. There are many cases that would have to come before you.'

'Oh I have the money,' said May, patting her handbag. She felt nervous but relieved at the same time. Almost exhilarated. It was working, the whole thing was actually moving. God bless Celia.

'It will be around £180 to £200, and in cash, you know that?'

'Yes, it's all here, but why should a well-known surgeon have to be paid in cash, Dr Harris? You know it makes it look a bit illegal and sort of underhand, doesn't it?'

Dr Harris smiled a tired smile. 'You ask me why he has to be paid in cash. Because he says so. Why he says so, I don't know. Maybe it's because some of his clients don't feel too like paying him after the event. It's not like plastic surgery or a broken leg, where they can see the results. In a termination you see no results. Maybe people don't pay so easily then. Maybe also Mr White doesn't have a warm relationship with his Income Tax people. I don't know.'

'Do I owe you anything?' May asked, putting on her coat.

'No, my dear, nothing.' He smiled and showed her to the door.

'It feels wrong. I'm used to paying a doctor at home or they send bills,' she said.

'Send me a picture postcard of your nice country sometime,' he said. 'When my wife was alive she and I spent several happy holidays there before all this business started.' He waved a hand to take in the course of Anglo-Irish politics and difficulties over the last ten years.

May blinked a bit hard and thanked him. She took a taxi which was passing his door and went to Oxford Street. She wanted to see what was in the shops because she was going to pretend that she had spent £200 on clothes and then they had all been lost or stolen. She hadn't yet worked out the details of this deception, which seemed unimportant compared to all the rest that had to be gone through. But she would need to know what was in the shops so that she could say what she was meant to have bought.

Imagining that she had this kind of money to spend, she examined jackets, skirts, sweaters, and the loveliest boots she had ever seen. If only she didn't have to throw this money away, she could have these things. It was her savings over ten months, she put by £30 a month with difficulty. Would Andy have liked her in the boots? She didn't know. He never said much about the way she looked. He saw her mostly in uniform when she could steal time to go to the flat he had for himself in the hotel. On the evenings when he was meant to be working late, and she was in fact cooking for him, she usually wore a dressing-gown, a long velvet one. Perhaps she might have bought a dressing-gown. She examined some, beautiful Indian silks, and a Japanese satin one in pink covered with little black butterflies. Yes, she would tell him she had bought that, he would like the sound of it, and be sorry it had been stolen.

She had a cup of coffee in one of the big shops and watched the other shoppers resting between bouts of buying. She wondered, did any of them look at her, and if so, would they know in a million years that her shopping money would remain in her purse until it was handed over to a Mr White so that he could abort Andy's baby? Why did she use words like that, why did she say things to hurt herself, she must have a very deep-seated sense of guilt.

14

Perhaps, she thought to herself with a bit of humour, she should save another couple of hundred pounds and come over for a few sessions with a Harley Street shrink. That should set her right.

It wasn't a long walk to Mr White's rooms, it wasn't a pleasant welcome. A kind of girl that May had before only seen in the pages of fashion magazines, bored, disdainful, elegant, reluctantly admitted her.

'Oh yes, Dr Harris's patient,' she said, as if May should have come in some tradesman's entrance. She felt furious, and inferior, and sat with her hands in small tight balls, and her eyes unseeing in the waiting-room.

Mr White looked like a caricature of a diplomat. He had elegant grey hair, elegant manicured hands. He moved very gracefully, he talked in practised, concerned clichés, he knew how to put people at their ease, and despite herself, and while still disliking him, May felt safe.

Another examination, another confirmation, more checking of dates. Good, good, she had come in plenty of time, sensible girl. No reasons she would like to discuss about whether this was the right course of action? No? Oh well, grown-up lady, must make up her own mind. Absolutely certain then? Fine, fine. A look at a big leather-bound book on his desk, a look at a small notebook. Leather-bound for the tax people, small notebook for himself, thought May viciously. Splendid, splendid. Tomorrow morning then, not a problem in the world, once she was sure, then he knew this was the best, and wisest thing. Very sad the people who dithered.

May could never imagine this man having dithered in his life. She was asked to see Vanessa on the way out. She knew that the girl would be called something like Vanessa.

Vanessa yawned and took £194 from her. She seemed to have difficulty in finding the six pounds in change. May wondered wildly whether this was meant to be a tip. If so, she would wait for a year until Vanessa found the change. With the notes came a discreet printed card advertising a nursing home on the other side of London.

'Before nine, fasting, just the usual overnight things,' said Vanessa helpfully.

'Tomorrow morning?' checked May.

'Well yes, naturally. You'll be out at eight the following

15

morning. They'll arrange everything like taxis. They have super food,' she added as an afterthought.

'They'd need to have for this money,' said May spiritedly.

'You're not just paying for the food,' said Vanessa wisely.

It was still raining. She rang Celia from a public phone-box. Everything was organized, she told her. Would Celia like to come and have a meal somewhere, and maybe they could go on to a theatre?

Celia was sorry, she had to work late, and she had already bought liver and bacon for supper. Could she meet May at home around nine? There was a great quiz show on telly, it would be a shame to miss it.

May went to a hairdresser and spent four times what she would have spent at home on a hair-do.

She went to a cinema and saw a film which looked as if it were going to be about a lot of sophisticated witty French people on a yacht and turned out to be about a sophisticated witty French girl who fell in love with the deck-hand on the yacht and when she purposely got pregnant, in order that he would marry her, he laughed at her and the witty sophisticated girl threw herself overboard. Great choice that, May said glumly, as she dived into the underground to go back to the smell of liver frying.

Celia asked little about the arrangements for the morning, only practical things like the address so that she could work out how long it would take to get there.

'Would you like me to come and see you?' she asked. 'I expect when it's all over, all finished you know, they'd let you have visitors. I could come after work.'

She emphasized the word 'could' very slightly. May immediately felt mutinous. She would love Celia to come, but not if it was going to be a duty, something she felt she had to do, against her principles, her inclinations.

'No, don't do that,' she said in a falsely bright voice. 'They have telly in the rooms apparently, and anyway, it's not as if I were going to be there for more than twenty-four hours.'

Celia looked relieved. She worked out taxi times and locations and turned on the quiz show.

In the half light May looked at her. She was unbending,

Celia was. She would survive everything, even the fact that Martin would never marry her. Christ, the whole thing was a mess. Why did people start life with such hopes, and as early as their mid-twenties become beaten and accepting of things. Was the rest of life going to be like this?

She didn't sleep so well, and it was a relief when Celia shouted that it was seven o'clock.

Wednesday. An ordinary Wednesday for the taxi-driver, who shouted some kind of amiable conversation at her. She missed most of it, because of the noise of the engine, and didn't bother to answer him half the time except with a grunt.

The place had creeper on the walls. It was a big house, with a small garden, and an attractive brass handle on the door. The nurse who opened it was Irish. She checked May's name on a list. Thank God it was O'Connor, there were a million O'Connors. Suppose she had had an unusual name, she'd have been found out immediately.

The bedroom was big and bright. Two beds, flowery covers, nice furniture. A magazine rack, a bookshelf. A television, a bathroom.

The Irish nurse offered her a hanger from the wardrobe for her coat as if this was a pleasant family hotel of great class and comfort. May felt frightened for the first time. She longed to sit down on one of the beds and cry, and for the nurse to put her arm around her and give her a cigarette and say that it would be all right. She hated being so alone.

The nurse was distant.

'The other lady will be in shortly. Her name is Miss Adams. She just went downstairs to say goodbye to her friend. If there's anything you'd like, please ring.'

She was gone, and May paced the room like a captured animal. Was she to undress? It was ridiculous to go to bed. You only went to bed in the day-time if you were ill. She was well, perfectly well.

Miss Adams burst in the door. She was a chubby, pretty girl about twenty-three. She was Australian, and her name was Hell, short for Helen.

'Come on, bedtime,' she said, and they both put on their nightdresses and got into beds facing each other. May had never felt so silly in her whole life.

17

'Are you sure we're meant to do this?' she asked.

'Positive,' Helen announced. 'I was here last year. They'll be in with the screens for modesty, the examination, and the pre-med. They go mad if you're not in bed. Of course that stupid Paddy of a nurse didn't tell you, they expect you to be inspired.'

Hell was right. In five minutes, the nurse and Mr White came in. A younger nurse carried a screen. Hell was examined first, then May, for blood pressure and temperature, and that kind of thing. Mr White was charming. He called her Miss O'Connor, as if he had known her all his life.

He patted her shoulder and told her she didn't have anything to worry about. The Irish nurse gave her an unsmiling injection which was going to make her drowsy. It didn't immediately.

Hell was doing her nails.

'You were really here last year?' asked May in disbelief.

'Yeah, there's nothing to it. I'll be back at work tomorrow.'

'Why didn't you take the Pill?' May asked.

'Why didn't you?' countered Hell.

'Well, I did for a bit, but I thought it was making me fat, and then anyway, you know, I thought I'd escaped for so long before I started the Pill that it would be all right. I was wrong.'

'I know.' Hell was sympathetic. 'I can't take it. I've got varicose veins already and I don't really understand all those things they give you in the Family Planning clinics, jellies, and rubber things, and diaphragms. It's worse than working out income tax. Anyway, you never have time to set up a scene like that before going to bed with someone, do you? It's like preparing for a battle.'

May laughed.

'It's going to be fine, love,' said Hell. 'Look, I know, I've been here before. Some of my friends have had it done four or five times. I promise you, it's only the people who don't know who worry. This afternoon you'll wonder what you were thinking about to look so white. Now if it had been terrible, would I be here again?'

'But your varicose veins?' said May, feeling a little sleepy.

'Go to sleep, kid,' said Hell. 'We'll have a chat when it's all over.'

Then she was getting onto a trolley, half-asleep, and going down corridors with lovely prints on the walls to a room with a lot of light, and transferring onto another table. She felt as if she could sleep for ever and she hadn't even had the anaesthetic yet. Mr White stood there in a coat brighter than his name. Someone was dressing him up the way they do in films.

She thought about Andy. 'I love you,' she said suddenly.

'Of course you do,' said Mr White, coming over and patting her kindly without a trace of embarrassment.

Then she was being moved again, she thought they hadn't got her right on the operating table, but it wasn't that, it was back into her own bed and more sleep.

There was a tinkle of china. Hell called over from the window.

'Come on, they've brought us some nice soup. Broth they call it.'

May blinked.

'Come on, May. I was done after you and I'm wide awake. Now didn't I tell you there was nothing to it?'

May sat up. No pain, no tearing feeling in her insides. No sickness.

'Are you sure they did me?' she asked.

They both laughed.

They had what the nursing-home called a light lunch. Then they got a menu so that they could choose dinner.

'There are some things that England does really well, and this is one of them,' Hell said approvingly, trying to decide between the delights that were offered. 'They even give us a small carafe of wine. If you want more you have to pay for it. But they kind of disapprove of us getting pissed.'

Hell's friend Charlie was coming in at six when he finished work. Would May be having a friend too, she wondered? No. Celia wouldn't come.

'I don't mean Celia,' said Hell. 'I mean the bloke.'

'He doesn't know, he's in Dublin, and he's married,' said May.

'Well, Charlie's married, but he bloody knows, and he'd know if he were on the moon.'

'It's different.'

'No, it's not different. It's the same for everyone, there are rules, you're a fool to break them. Didn't he pay for it either, this guy?'

'No. I told you he doesn't know.'

'Aren't you noble,' said Hell scornfully. 'Aren't you a real Lady Galahad. Just visiting London for a day or two, darling, just going to see a few friends, see you soon. Love you darling. Is that it?'

'We don't go in for so many darlings as that in Dublin,' said May.

'You don't go in for much common sense either. What will you gain, what will he gain, what will anyone gain? You come home penniless, a bit lonely. He doesn't know what the hell you've been doing, he isn't extra-sensitive and loving and grateful because he doesn't have anything to be grateful about as far as he's concerned.'

'I couldn't tell him. I couldn't. I couldn't ask him for £200 and say what it was for. That wasn't in the bargain, that was never part of the deal.'

May was almost tearful, mainly from jealousy she thought. She couldn't bear Hell's Charlie to come in, while her Andy was going home to his wife because there would be nobody to cook him something exciting and go to bed with him in his little manager's flat.

'When you go back, tell him. That's my advice,' said Hell. 'Tell him you didn't want to worry him, you did it all on your own because the responsibility was yours since you didn't take the Pill. That's unless you think he'd have wanted it?'

'No, he wouldn't have wanted it.'

'Well then, that's what you do. Don't ask him for the money straight out, just let him know you're broke. He'll react some way then. It's silly not to tell them at all. My sister did that with her bloke back in Melbourne. She never told him at all, and she got upset because he didn't know the sacrifice she had made, and every time she bought a drink or paid for a cinema ticket she got resentful of him. All for no reason, because he didn't bloody know.'

'I might,' said May, but she knew she wouldn't.

Charlie came in. He was great fun, very fond of Hell, wanting to be sure she was okay, and no problems. He brought a bottle of wine which they shared, and he told them funny stories about what had happened at the office. He was in advertising. He arranged to meet Hell for lunch next day and joked his way out of the room.

'He's a lovely man,' said May.

'Old Charlie's smashing,' agreed Hell. He had gone back home to entertain his wife and six dinner guests. His wife was a marvellous hostess apparently. They were always having dinner parties.

'Do you think he'll ever leave her?' asked May.

'He'd be out of his brains if he did,' said Hell cheerfully.

May was thoughtful. Maybe everyone would be out of their brains if they left good, comfortable, happy home set-ups for whatever the other woman imagined she could offer. She wished she could be as happy as Hell.

'Tell me about your fellow,' Hell said kindly.

May did, the whole long tale. It was great to have somebody to listen, somebody who didn't say she was on a collision course, somebody who didn't purse up lips like Celia, someone who said, 'Go on, what did you do then?'

'He sounds like a great guy,' said Hell, and May smiled happily.

They exchanged addresses, and Hell promised that if ever she came to Ireland she wouldn't ring up the hotel and say, 'Can I talk to May, the girl I had the abortion with last winter?' and they finished Charlie's wine, and went to sleep.

The beds were stripped early next morning when the final examination had been done, and both were pronounced perfect and ready to leave. May wondered fancifully how many strange life stories the room must have seen.

'Do people come here for other reasons apart from ... er, terminations?' she asked the disapproving Irish nurse.

'Oh certainly they do, you couldn't work here otherwise,' said the nurse. 'It would be like a death factory, wouldn't it?'

That puts me in my place, thought May, wondering why she hadn't the courage to say that she was only visiting the home, she didn't earn her living from it.

She let herself into Celia's gloomy flat. It had become gloomy again like the way she had imagined it before she

21

saw it. The warmth of her first night there was gone. She looked around and wondered why Celia had no pictures, no books, no souvenirs.

There was a note on the telephone pad.

'I didn't ring or anything, because I forgot to ask if you had given your real name, and I wouldn't know who to ask for. Hope you feel well again. I'll be getting some chicken pieces so we can have supper together around 8. Ring me if you need me. C.'

May thought for a bit. She went out and bought Celia a casserole dish, a nice one made of cast-iron. It would be useful for all those little high-protein, low-calorie dinners Celia cooked. She also bought a bunch of flowers, but could find no vase when she came back and had to use a big glass instead. She left a note thanking her for the hospitality, warm enough to sound properly grateful, and a genuinely warm remark about how glad she was that she had been able to do it all through nice Dr Harris. She said nothing about the time in the nursing-home. Celia would prefer not to know. May just said that she was fine, and thought she would go back to Dublin tonight. She rang the airline and booked a plane.

Should she ring Celia and tell her to get only one chicken piece. No, damn Celia, she wasn't going to ring her. She had a fridge, hadn't she?

The plane didn't leave until the early afternoon. For a wild moment she thought of joining Hell and Charlie in the pub where they were meeting, but dismissed the idea. She must now make a list of what clothes she was meant to have bought and work out a story about how they had disappeared. Nothing that would make Andy get in touch with police or airlines to find them for her. It was going to be quite hard, but she'd have to give Andy some explanation of what she'd been doing, wouldn't she? And he would want to know why she had spent all that money. Or would he? Did he even know she had all that money? She couldn't remember telling him. He wasn't very interested in her little savings, they talked more about his investments. And she must remember that if he was busy or cross tonight or tomorrow she wasn't to take it out on him. Like Hell had said, there wasn't any point in her expecting a bit of cossetting when he didn't even know she needed it.

How sad and lonely it would be to live like Celia, to be so suspicious of men, to think so ill of Andy. Celia always said he was selfish and just took what he could get. That was typical of Celia, she understood nothing. Hell had understood more, in a couple of hours, than Celia had in three years. Hell knew what it was like to love someone.

But May didn't think Hell had got it right about telling Andy all about the abortion. Andy might be against that kind of thing. He was very moral in his own way, was Andy.

Holland Park

Everyone hated Malcolm and Melissa out in Greece last summer. They pretended they thought they were marvellous, but deep down we really hated them. They were too perfect, too bright, intelligent, witty and aware. They never monopolized conversations in the taverna, they never seemed to impose their will on anyone else, but somehow we all ended up doing what they wanted to do. They didn't seem lovey-dovey with each other, but they had a companionship which drove us all to a frenzy of rage.

I nearly fainted when I got a note from them six months later. I thought they were the kind of people who wrote down addresses as a matter of courtesy, and you never heard from them again.

'I hate trying to recreate summer madness,' wrote Melissa. 'So I won't gather everyone from the Hellenic scene, but Malcolm and I would be thrilled if you could come to supper on the 20th. Around eightish, very informal and everything. We've been so long out of touch that I don't know if there's anyone I should ask you to bring along; if so, of course the invitation is for two. Give me a ring sometime so that I'll know how many strands of spaghetti to put in the pot. It will be super to see you again.'

I felt that deep down she knew there was nobody she should ask me to bring along. She wouldn't need to hire a private detective for that, Melissa would know. The wild notion of hiring someone splendid from an escort agency

24

came and went. In three artless questions Melissa would find out where he was from, and think it was a marvellous fun thing to have done.

I didn't believe her about the spaghetti, either. It would be something that looked effortless but would be magnificent and unusual at the same time. Perhaps a perfect Greek meal for nostalgia, where she would have made all the hard things like pitta and humus and fetta herself, and laugh away the idea that it was difficult. Or it would be a dinner around a mahogany table with lots of cut-glass decanters, and a Swiss darling to serve it and wash up.

But if I didn't go, Alice would kill me, and Alice and I often had a laugh over the perfection of Malcolm and Melissa. She said I had made them up, and that the people in the photos were in fact models who had been hired by the Greek Tourist Board to make the place look more glamorous. Their names had passed into our private shorthand. Alice would describe a restaurant as a 'Malcolm and Melissa sort of place', meaning that it was perfect, understated and somehow irritating at the same time. I would say that I had handled a situation in a 'Malcolm and Melissa way', meaning that I had scored without seeming to have done so at all.

So I rang the number and Melissa was delighted to hear from me. Yes, didn't Greece all seem like a dream nowadays, and wouldn't it be foolish to go to the same place next year in case it wasn't as good, and no, they hadn't really decided where to go next year, but Malcolm had seen this advertisement about a yacht party which wanted a few more people to make up the numbers, and it might be fun, but one never knew and one was a bit trapped on a yacht if it was all terrible. And super that I could come on the 20th, and then with the voice politely questioning, would I be bringing anyone else?

In one swift moment I made a decision. 'Well, if it's not going to make it too many I would like to bring this friend of mine, Alice,' I said, and felt a roaring in my ears as I said it. Melissa was equal to anything.

'Of course, of course, that's lovely, we look forward to meeting her. See you both about eightish then. It's not far from the tube, but maybe you want to get a bus, I'm not sure . . .'

'Alice has a car,' I said proudly.

'Oh, better still. Tell her there's no problem about parking, we have a bit of waste land around the steps. It makes life heavenly in London not to have to worry about friends parking.'

Alice was delighted. She said she hoped they wouldn't turn out to have terrible feet of clay and that we would have to find new names for them. I was suddenly taken with a great desire to impress her with them, and an equal hope that they would find her as funny and witty as I did. Alice can be eccentric at times, she can go into deep silences. We giggled a lot about what we'd wear. Alice said that we should go in full evening dress, with capes, and embroidered handbags, and cigarette-holders, but I said that would be ridiculous.

'It would make her uneasy,' said Alice with an evil face.

'But she's not horrible, she's nice. She's asked us to dinner, she'll be very nice,' I pleaded.

'I thought you couldn't stand her,' said Alice, disappointed.

'It's hard to explain. She doesn't mean any harm, she just does everything too well.' I felt immediately that I was taking the myth away from Malcolm and Melissa and wished I'd never thought of asking Alice.

Between then and the 20th, Alice thought that we should go in boiler suits, in tennis gear, dressed as Greek peasants, and at one stage that we should dress up as nuns and tell her that this was what we were in real life. With difficulty I managed to persuade her that we were not to look on the evening as some kind of search-and-destroy mission, and Alice reluctantly agreed.

I don't really know why we had allowed the beautiful couple to become so much part of our fantasy life. It wasn't as if we had nothing else to think about. Alice was a solicitor with a busy practice consisting mainly of battered wives, worried one-parent families faced with eviction, and a large vocal section of the female population who felt that they had been discriminated against in their jobs. She had an unsatisfactory love-life going on with one of the partners in the firm, usually when his wife was in hospital, which didn't make her feel at all guilty, she saw it more as a kind of service that she was offering. I work in a theatre writing publicity-handouts and arranging news-paper interviews for the stars, and in my own way I meet plenty of glittering people. I sort of love a hopeless man who is a good writer but a bad person to love, since he loves too many people, but it doesn't break my heart.

I don't suppose that deep down Alice and I want to live in a big house in Holland Park, and be very beautiful and charming, and have a worthy job like Melissa raising money for a good cause, and be married to a very bright, sunny-looking man like Malcolm, who runs a left-wing bookshop that somehow has made him a great deal of money. I don't *suppose* we could have been directly envious. More indirectly irritated, I would have thought.

I was very irritated with myself on the night of the 20th because I changed five times before Alice came to collect me. The black sweater and skirt looked too severe, the gingham dress mutton dressed as lamb, the yellow too garish, the pink too virginal. I settled for a tapestry skirt and a cheap cotton top.

'Christ, you look like a suite of furniture,' said Alice when she arrived.

'Do I? Is it terrible?' I asked, anxious as a sixteen-year-old before a first dance.

'No, of course it isn't,' said Alice. 'It's fine, it's just a bit sort of sofa-coverish if you know what I mean. Let's hope it clashes with her décor.'

Tears of rage in my eyes, I rushed into the bedroom and put on the severe black again. Safe, is what magazines call black. Safe I would be.

Alice was very contrite.

'I'm sorry, I really am. I don't know why I said that, it looked fine. I've never given two minutes' thought to clothes, you know that. Oh for God's sake wear it, please. Take off the mourning gear and put on what you were wearing.'

'Does this look like mourning then?' I asked, riddled with anxiety.

'Give me a drink,' said Alice firmly. 'In ten years of knowing each other we have never had to waste three minutes talking about clothes. Why are we doing it to-night?'

I poured her a large Scotch and one for me, and put on

a jokey necklace which took the severe look away from the black. Alice said it looked smashing.

Alice told me about a client whose husband had put Vim in her tin of tooth powder and she had tried to convince herself that he still wasn't too bad. I told Alice about an ageing actress who was opening next week in a play, and nobody, not even the man I half love, would do an interview with her for any paper because they said, quite rightly, that she was an old bore. We had another Scotch to reflect on all that.

I told Alice about the man I half loved having asked me to go to Paris with him next weekend, and Alice said I should tell him to get stuffed, unless, of course, he was going to pay for the trip, in which case I must bring a whole lot of different judgements to bear. She said she was going to withdraw part of her own services from her unsatisfactory partner, because the last night they had spent together had been a perusal of *The Home Doctor* to try and identify the nature of his wife's illness. I said I thought his wife's illness might be deeply rooted in drink, and Alice said I could be right but it wasn't the kind of thing you said to someone's husband. Talking about drink reminded us to have another and then we grudgingly agreed it was time to go.

There were four cars in what Melissa had described as a bit of waste land, an elegantly paved semi-circular courtyard in front of the twelve steps up to the door. Alice commented that they were all this year's models, and none of them cost a penny under three thousand. She parked her battered 1969 Volkswagen in the middle, where it looked like a small child between a group of elegant adults.

Malcolm opened the door, glass in hand. He was so pleased to see us that I wondered how he had lived six months without the experience. Oh come on, I told myself, that's being unfair, if he wasn't nice and welcoming I would have more complaints. The whole place looked like the film set for a trendy frothy movie on gracious modern living. Melissa rushed out in a tapestry skirt, and I nearly cried with relief that I hadn't worn mine. Melissa is shaped like a pencil rather than a sofa; the contrast would have been mind-blowing.

We were wafted into a sitting-room, and wafted is the

word. Nobody said 'come this way' or 'let me introduce you' but somehow there we were with drinks in our hands, sitting between other people, whose names had been said clearly, a Melissa would never mutter. The drinks were good and strong, a Malcolm would never be mean. Low in the background a record-player had some nostalgic songs from the Sixties, the time when we had all been young and impressionable, none of your classical music, nor your songs of the moment. Malcolm and Melissa couldn't be obvious if they tried.

And it was like being back in Andrea's Taverna again. Everyone felt more witty and relaxed because Malcolm and Melissa were there, sort of in charge of things without appearing to be. They sat and chatted, they didn't fuss, they never tried to drag anyone into the conversation or to force some grounds of common interest. Just because we were all there together under their roof ... that was enough.

And it seemed to be enough for everyone. A great glow came over the group in the sunset, and the glow deepened when a huge plate of spaghetti was served. It was spaghetti, damn her. But not the kind that you and I would ever make. Melissa seemed to be out of the room only three minutes, and I know it takes at least eight to cook the pasta. But there it was, excellent, mountainous, with garlic bread, fresh and garlicky, not the kind that breaks your teeth on the outside and then is soggy within. The salad was like an exotic still-life, it had everything in it except lettuce. People moved as if in a dance to the table. There were no cries of praise and screams of disclaimer from the hostess. Why then should I have been so resentful of it all?

Alice seemed to be loving every minute of her evening, she had already fought with Malcolm about the kind of women's literature he sold, but it was a happy fight where she listened to the points he was making and answered them. If she didn't like someone she wouldn't bother to do this. She had been talking to Melissa about some famous woman whom they both knew through work, and they were giggling about the famous woman's shortcomings. Alice was forgetting her role, she was breaking the rules. She had come to understand more about the Melissa and Malcolm people so that we could laugh at them. Instead, she looked in grave danger of getting on with them.

I barely heard what someone called Keith was saying to me about my theatre. I realized with a great shock that I was jealous. Jealous that Alice was having such a nice time, and impressing Melissa and Malcolm just because she was obviously not trying to.

This shock was so physical that a piece of something exotic, avocado maybe, anyway something that shouldn't be in a salad, got stuck in my throat. No amount of clearing and hurrumphing could get rid of it and I stood up in a slight panic.

Alice grasped at once.

'Relax and it will go down,' she called. 'Just force your limbs to relax, and your throat will stop constricting. No, don't bang her, there's no need.'

She spoke with such confidence that I tried to make my hands and knees feel heavy, and miracles it worked.

'That's a good technique,' said Malcolm admiringly, when I had been patted down and, scarlet with rage, assured everyone I was fine.

'It's very unscientific,' said the doctor amongst us, who would have liked the chance to slit my throat and remove the object to cries of admiration.

'It worked,' said Alice simply.

The choking had gone away but not the reason for it. Why did I suddenly feel so possessive about Alice, so hurt when she hadn't liked my dress, so jealous and envious that she was accepted here on her own terms and not as my friend? It was ridiculous. Sometimes I didn't hear from Alice for a couple of weeks; we weren't soul mates over everything, just long-standing friends.

'. . . have you had this flat in the City long?' asked Keith politely.

'Oh that's not my flat, that's Alice's,' I said. Alice was always unusual. She had thought that since the City would be deserted at weekends, the time she wanted a bit of peace, that's where she should live. And of course it worked. Not a dog barked, not a child cried, not a car revved up when Alice was sleeping till noon on a Sunday.

'No, I live in Fulham,' I said, thinking how dull and predictable it sounded.

'Oh I thought . . .' Keith didn't say what he thought

but he didn't ask about my flat in Fulham.

Malcolm was saying that Alice and I should think about the yachting holiday. Keith and Rosemary were thinking about it, weren't they? They were, and it would be great fun if we went as a six, then we could sort of take over in case the other people were ghastly.

'It sounds great,' I said dishonestly and politely. 'Yes, you must tell me more about it.'

'Weren't you meant to be going on holiday with old Thing?' said Alice practically.

'That was very vague,' I snapped. 'The weekend in Paris was definite but the holiday ... nothing was fixed. Anyway weren't you meant to be going to a cottage with your Thing...?'

Everyone looked at me, it was as if I had belched loudly or taken off my blouse unexpectedly. They were waiting for me to finish and in a well-bred way rather hoping that I wouldn't. Their eyes were like shouts of encouragement.

'You said that if his wife was put away for another couple of weeks you might go to their very unsocialistic second home? Didn't you?'

Alice laughed, everyone else looked stunned.

Melissa spooned out huge helpings of a ten thousand calorie ice-cream with no appearance of having noticed a social gaffe.

'Well, when the two of you make up your minds, do tell us,' she said. 'It would be great fun, and we have to let these guys know by the end of the month, apparently. They sound very nice actually. Jeremy and Jacky they're called, he makes jewellery and Jacky is an artist. They've lots of other friends going too, a couple of girls who work with Jeremy and their boy friends, I think. It's just Jeremy and Jacky who are ... who are organizing it all.'

Like a flash I saw it. Melissa thought Alice and I were lesbians. She was being her usual tolerant liberated self over it all. If you like people, what they do in bed is none of your business. HOW could she be so crass as to think that about Alice and myself? My face burned with rage. Slowly like heavy flowers falling off a tree came all the reasons. I was dressed so severely, I had asked could I bring a woman not a man to her party, I had been manless in Greece when she met me the first time, I had just put on this appalling show of spitely spiteful dikey jealousy about Alice's relationship with a man. Oh God. Oh God.

I knew little or nothing about lesbians. Except that they were different. I never was friendly with anyone who was one. I knew they didn't wear bowler hats, but I thought that they did go in for this aggressive sort of picking on one another in public. Oh God.

Alice was talking away about the boat with interest. How much would it cost? Who decided where and when they would stop? Did Jeremy and Jacky sound madly camp and would they drive everyone mad looking for sprigs of tarragon in case the pot au feu was ruined?

Everyone was laughing, and Malcolm was being liberated and tolerant and left-wing.

'Come on Alice, nothing wrong with tarragon, nothing wrong with fussing about food, we all fuss about something. Anyway, they didn't say anything to make us think that they would fuss about food, stop typecasting.'

He said it in a knowing way. I felt with a sick dread that he could have gone on and said, 'After all, I don't typecast you and expect you to wear a hairnet and military jacket.'

I looked at Alice, her thin white face all lit up laughing. Of course I felt strongly about her, she was my friend. She was very important to me, I didn't need to act with Alice. I resented the way the awful man with his alcoholic wife treated her, but was never jealous of him because Alice didn't really give her mind to him. And as for giving anything else ... well I suppose they made a lot of love together but so did I and the unsatisfactory journalist. I didn't want Alice in that way. I mean that was madness, we wouldn't even know what to do. We would laugh ourselves silly.

Kiss Alice?

Run and lay my head on Alice's breast?

Have Alice stroke my hair?

That's what people who were in love did. We didn't do that.

Did Alice need me? Yes, of course she did. She often told me that I was the only bit of sanity in her life, that I was safe. I had known her for ten years, hardly anyone else she knew nowadays went back that far.

Malcolm filled my coffee cup.

'Do persuade her to come with us,' he said gently to me. 'She's marvellous really, and I know you'd both enjoy yourselves.'

I looked at him like a wild animal. I saw us fitting into their lives, another splendid liberal concept, slightly racy, perfectly acceptable. 'We went on holiday with that super gay couple, most marvellous company, terribly entertaining.' Which of us would he refer to as the He? Would there be awful things like leaving us alone . together, or nodding tolerantly over our little rows?

The evening and not only the evening stretched ahead in horror. Alice had been laying into the wine, would she be able to drive? If not, oh God, would they offer us a double bed in some spare room in this mansion? Would they suggest a taxi home to Fulham since my place was nearer? Would they speculate afterwards why we kept two separate establishments in the first place?

Worse, would I ever be able to laugh with Alice about it or was it too important? I might disgust her, alarm her, turn her against me. I might unleash all kinds of love that she had for me deep down, and how would I handle that?

Of course I loved Alice, I just didn't realize it. But what lover, what poor unfortunate lover in the history of the whole damn thing, ever had the tragedy of Coming Out in Malcolm and Melissa's lovely home in Holland Park?

Notting Hill Gate

Everyone knew that Daphne's friend Mike was a shit and to give us our due most of us said so. But she laughed and said we were full of rubbish. She agreed, still laughing, to take the address of the battered wife place, just in case, then we gave her a lovely fur jacket that Mike wouldn't be able to share, and she left us and married him. We never saw her again. But we had to find a new secretary.

Nowadays nobody thinks any more that you meet a lot of interesting people on a newspaper, so you don't have breathless, over-educated, anxious-to-please Oxford graduates rushing around doing all the dirty work willingly as well as all the ordinary work efficiently. Nowadays you have temps earning a fortune, but with no security, and no plans and no interest in what they're doing. My woolly, right-minded, left-thinking views thought that this was unfair on the girls ... they had no career structure, no dignity, and the agencies made all the money. But then from time to time my wrong-minded right-wing views made me wonder what the country was coming to when you couldn't get a girl who could spell, read, take orders and be grateful for a good job. It was a month of temps before Rita came.

Rita was big and black and tough about luncheon-vouchers, and wanted us to buy her a season ticket on the tube. She walked not like other people walk ... she rolled along as if she had wheels in her shoes. She had a lot of low-cut purple or green blouses and she wore a series of desperately tight orange or yellow skirts. Marian, who deals with readers' letters, said she thought that Rita's skirts must rip open every evening after the strain of the day, and she would throw them away.

She looked slow and lazy, and as if she was thinking of something else almost all the time, but she was far better than anyone we had had up until then. You didn't have to tell Rita twice that there were ten hopeless people who kept coming into the office with ideas for stories, and that none of the ideas were ever any use. Rita just nodded vaguely, but she knew how to deal with them. She would write down what they said, type it out and put it in a file. The people would go away satisfied that things were under-way, and Rita had all the ideas neatly put in the H file, under Hopeless.

After three weeks, we realized two things, firstly that Rita was still there, that she hadn't walked out at 11 a.m. one day like the other temps were in the habit of doing, and secondly that she didn't need to be watched and ad-vised all the time. Martin, the features editor, asked her if she would like a permanent job, and Rita looked as if she had been offered a potato crisp at a bus-stop, and said she might as well. But only if he would pay for a monthly ticket on the underground for her.

Rita lived in Notting Hill but that's all she said. This was a change too, because normally whoever sat in that desk seemed to unburden themselves of a long and com-plicated life history. There was nothing about Daphne's Mike that we didn't know, his deprived childhood, his poor relationship with Daphne's mother, his disastrous early marriage . . . even Daphne's black eyes were explained away by some incredible misunderstanding, some terrible mistake for which Mike was now heart-broken. All the useless temps had told us tales about their flats being too far out, or their fellows thinking they owned them, or dis-tant boyfriends in Cumbria or on sheep-stations in Austra-lia who wanted them to throw up the job and come home and marry them. Rita never told us anything.

'Do you live in a flat or with your family?' Marian asked her once.

'Why?' asked Rita.

'Oh well I just wondered,' said Marian a bit confused.

'Oh that's all right,' said Rita quite happily, but didn't answer the question.

She used her luncheon-vouchers to buy a huge sandwich and a carton of milk, and she ate it quietly reading a trashy magazine, or at least one that was marginally more trashy than our own features pages. Because she was so uncommunicative, I suppose we were more interested in her. She got the odd phone call, and I found myself listening to her side of the conversation with all the attention of a village postmistress. She would speak in her slow flat tone, smiling only rarely, and seemed to be agreeing with whoever was on the other end about some course of action.

Once she said, 'He's a bad bastard I tell you, he used to be a friend of my husband . . . get out of it if you can.' Full of secret information I told Marian and the others that Rita had a husband. Martin said he had always supposed she did; nothing about Rita would suggest she was a lonely girl who went home to an empty bed, she was too sexy. We had long arguments about his attitudes, like that only sexy women had husbands and that all single women went home to empty beds . . . but it was an old and well worn line of argument. I was more interested that he thought Rita sexy. I thought she was overblown, and fat, and very gaudily dressed, but assumed that West Indians might like brighter colours than we would because of all their bright sunlight back home. Sexy. No.

I was waiting one night in a pub for my sister who's always late and I had forgotten to bring anything to read. So I looked around hopefully in case anyone had abandoned an evening paper. There was one on the floor near a very good-looking blond lad and I went over to pick it up. He put his foot on it immediately.

'That's mine,' he said.

He was very drunk. When someone's very drunk you don't make an issue about nicking their evening paper. I apologized and said I thought it was one that someone had finished with. He looked at me coldly and forgave me. Irritated, I went back to my seat and wished that my sister could for once in her life turn up at something approaching the time arranged. The blond boy now stumbled over to my table and in exaggerated gestures began to present me the paper. He managed to knock my gin and tonic over my skirt and the contents of the ashtray on top of that. I could have killed him I was so annoyed, but before I had time to do anything, a big shadow fell on the whole scene. It was of all people Rita.

She didn't seem embarrassed, surprised, or apologetic. She said, 'You drunken bum,' pulled him away back to a distant seat, ordered me another gin and tonic, brought a cloth, and a lot of paper napkins, all in what looked like slow movements, but they only took a minute or two all the same.

I was so surprised to see her that I forgot about the disgusting mess seeping into my best cream-coloured linen skirt. What was even more amazing, she offered no explanation. I'd have said I was sorry about my friend, or made some nervous joke about it being a small world. Rita just said, 'Hot water, and if that doesn't work, dry cleaning tomorrow, I suppose.' She said it in exactly the same way she'd say, 'We can try the usual photographer for the fashion pictures, and if he's busy get the agency ones I suppose.' With no involvement at all.

Hot water didn't work very well, the whole skirt now looked appalling. When my sister Trudy came in, I was in such a temper that it frightened her.

'You can wear a coat,' she said trying to placate me.

'I haven't got a bloody coat,' I said. 'It's the middle of bloody summer. My coat's at home on the other side of London, isn't it?'

Rita asked with the mild concern of a bystander and not the sense of responsibility of someone whose drunken boyfriend had just ruined an expensive skirt:

'Do you want something to wear? I'll give you something.'

Trudy thought she was an innocent concerned bystander and started to gush that it would be perfectly all right thank you . . .

Rita said, 'I live upstairs, you can come up and choose what you'd like.'

Now this was too good to miss. Firstly I had discovered that Rita had a white boyfriend who looked like a Greek God, that he was as drunk as a maggot, and that Rita lived over a pub. Now I was going to see her place . . . this would be a great dossier for the office.

'Thanks, Rita,' I said ungraciously, and left Trudy open-mouthed behind me.

As we went out the pub door and almost immediately through another, I wondered, Was I mad? Rita's clothes would go around me four times. How could she or I think that any skirt of hers would fit me?

She opened the door of a cheaply furnished, but neat and bright, apartment. Two small and very pigtailed girls sat on a big cushion looking at a big colour telly.

'This is Miss that I work with,' said Rita.

'Hallo Miss,' they chorused, and went back to looking at bionic things on the screen.

We walked into a bedroom also very neat and bright, and Rita opened a cupboard. She took out what looked like two yards of material with a ribbon around the top.

'It's a wrap-around skirt, it fits any size,' she said. I got out of the dirty dishcloth I was wearing, and wrapped it around, and tied the ribbon. It looked fine.

'Thank you very much indeed, Rita,' I said, trying at the same time to take in every detail for the telling tomorrow in the pub, while Rita would be sitting at her desk. There were big prints on the wall, Chinese girls, and horses with flying manes. The bed had a beautiful patchwork quilt, it looked as if it could sleep four people comfortably.

'Are those your little girls?' I asked, a question brought on indirectly by the bed I suppose.

'They're Martie and Anna, they live here,' said Rita.

I realized immediately she hadn't told me whether they were her daughters, her sisters, her nieces, or her friends. And I also realized that I wasn't going to ask any more.

'You can leave the other skirt,' said Rita and then, for the very first time volunteering some information, she added, 'Andrew has quite enough money to pay to have it dry-cleaned, and I'll bring it into the office for you on Friday.'

Oh, so he was called Andrew, the young beautiful boy, and he had plenty of money, oh ho. I was learning something anyway. I didn't dare to ask her whether he was her boyfriend. It wasn't that Rita was superior or distant, but she drew a shutter down like someone slamming a door, and didn't find it rude or impolite. It left you feeling rude and impolite instead.

I thanked her for the skirt. Martie and Anna said 'Goodbye Miss' without removing their eyes from the screen. Somehow *they* seemed so much at ease with the goings-on that it made me very annoyed with myself for feeling diffident because this was a black house and I was a white woman. Who creates these barriers anyway, I argued with myself, and, taking a deep breath, said to Rita on the stairs:

'Why do they wear their hair in those tight little pig-tails? They'd be much prettier if their hair was loose.'

'Maybe,' Rita shrugged, as if I had asked her why she didn't move the coffee percolator to another table in the office to give herself more room. 'Yeah maybe,' she agreed.

'Do you like them with their hair all tied up like that?' I asked courageously.

'Oh it has nothing to do with me,' she said, and we were out on the street and into the pub again.

Trudy had a face like thunder when I came back but she greeted Rita pleasantly enough, and asked her if she would like to join us.

Rita shook her head. 'This drunken baby has to be taken to bed,' she said enigmatically, and she frog-marched the handsome Andrew out the door without a good-bye. I ran to the window to see whether she was taking him up to her own flat, but they had gone too quickly. There was no way of knowing whether they had gone in her door or turned the corner, and I didn't really want to run out into the street to check.

Trudy wasn't very interested in my speculation.

'I don't suppose I should have been so surprised to see her,' I reflected. 'I knew she lived in Notting Hill. This is a very black area around here too, I suppose.'

'Quite a few white people live here as well,' said Trudy acidly, and I forgot that she had just paid what seemed like an enormous sum of money for a very small, very twee house around the corner.

The others were interested at lunch-time the next day. They wanted to know what Andrew looked like.

'Like that actor who plays the part of Henry in that

serial,' I said, meaning an actor whose dizzying looks had sent people of all ages into some kind of wistful speculation as to what a future with him might be like.

'You mean Andy Sparks,' said Marian, and with a thud I realized it *was* Andy Sparks. It was just that his face seemed so contorted, and he hadn't worn the boyish eager look nor the boyish eager anorak he always wore in the serial.

'My God, it was definitely him,' I said. By this time the others were losing interest, they thought I had gone into fantasy. Large lumbering black Rita, who read rubbishy magazines, who never seemed interested in anything, not even herself . . . she could never have been the petite amie of Andy Sparks.

'We did a feature on him about three weeks ago,' said Martin. 'No, it can't have been the same guy, you only think so because they had the same name.'

'You did say Rita was sexy,' I pointed out, trying to bolster up my claim that she might be so sexy that she could have been seen with the superstar of the moment.

'Not *that* sexy,' said Martin, and they began to talk about other things.

'Don't tell her I told you,' I said. I felt it was important that Rita shouldn't think I had been blabbing about her. It was as if I had gone into her territory by being in that pub, and I shouldn't be carrying back tales from it.

I looked up the back pages surreptitiously. It *was* the same guy. He had looked unhappy and drawn compared to the pictures we used of him, but it was the same Andrew.

On Friday Rita handed me a parcel and an envelope. The parcel was my skirt, which she said the cleaners had made a lovely balls of. They were sorry but with a stain like that it was owner's risk only, and she had alas agreed to owner's risk. They were, she said, the best cleaners around. I looked at the docket and saw she was right. I also saw the name on the docket. It said 'A. Sparks'. She took the docket away and gave me the envelope. It was a gift-token for almost exactly what the skirt had cost, and it was from the shop where I had in fact bought it. Not a big chain-store but a boutique.

'I can't take it,' I said.

'You might as well, he can afford it.' She shrugged.

'But if it had been a stranger, not a . . . er . . . well some-one you knew, then I wouldn't have got it replaced,' I stammered.

'That's your good luck, then,' said Rita and went back to her desk. She hadn't even left me the docket so that I could show the others I was right about the name.

At lunchtime I invited Rita out with me.

'I thought you were having lunch with that woman who wrote the book about flowers,' she said, neither interested nor bored, just stating a fact.

'She rang and cancelled,' I said.

'I didn't put her through to you,' said Rita.

'No, well I rang her on the direct line actually,' I said, furious to have my gesture of taking her out to lunch made into an issue. 'I didn't feel like talking to her.'

'And you feel like talking to me?' asked Rita with one of her rare smiles.

'I'd like to buy you a nice lunch and relax with you and thank you for going to all that trouble over my skirt,' I snapped. It sounded the most ungracious invitation to lunch ever given.

Even if I had been down on my knees with roses I don't think Rita would have reacted differently.

'Thanks very much, but I don't think I will. I don't like long boozy lunches. I have too much work to do in the afternoons here anyway.'

'For Christ's sake it doesn't have to be long and boozy, and though you may not have noticed it, I work here in the afternoons myself,' I said like a spoiled child.

'Okay then,' she said, took up her shoulder bag, and with no coat to cover her fat bouncing bottom and half-exposed large black breasts, she rolled down the corridor with me, into the lift and out into the street.

I chose a fairly posh place, I wasn't going to have her say I went to less expensive places with her than with the journalists or people I interviewed.

She looked at the menu as if it were a list of cuttings we needed her to get from the library. I asked her if she would like pâté and said that they made it very well here.

'Sure,' she said.

I could see it was going to be hard going.

We ordered one glass of wine each, she seemed to accept

41

that too as if it were extra dictation. The few starts I made
were doomed. When I asked her whether she found the
work interesting in the office, she said it was fine. Better
than where she had worked before? Oh yes she supposed
so. Where had that been? Hadn't I seen it on her applica-
tion? She'd been with a lot of firms as a temp. I was driven
to talk about the traffic in London, the refuge of all who
run out of conversation.

Just then a bird-brained rival of mine on another newspaper came over. Normally I would have walked under
buses to avoid her. Today she seemed like a rescue ship
sent to a desert island.

She sat down, had a glass of wine, wouldn't eat because
of some new diet, wouldn't take her coat off because she
was in a hurry, and looked at Rita with interest. I introduced them just name by name without saying where either
worked.

'I expect you're being interviewed,' the bird-brain,
highly-paid writer said to Rita. Rita shrugged. She wasn't
embarrassed, she wasn't waiting for me to give her a lead.
She shrugged because she couldn't be bothered to say anything.

At least now I didn't have to do all the talking. Rita and
I heard how hard life was, how long it took to get anywhere
these days because of the traffic, how hopeless hairdressers
were, how they never listened to what you wanted done,
how silly the new summer clothes were, how shoes didn't
last three months, how selfish show-biz people were making big productions out of being interviewed, instead of
being so grateful for all the free publicity. Then her eyes
brightened.

'I'm doing Andy Sparks,' she said. 'Yes I know, your lot
had him last week, but he's promised to tell me all about
his private life. I'm taking him to dinner in a little club
I've just joined, so that people won't keep coming over to
disturb us. He's meant to be absolutely as dumb as anything, only intelligent when he gets lines to read. Anyway
we'll see, we can't go far wrong if he tells a bit about the
loves of his life. I only hope it won't be religion or his
mother or a collie dog or something.'

Rita sat half-listening as she had been doing all along.
I started to say about three different things and got a

coughing fit. Finally it dawned on the world's most confident bad writer that she was losing her audience so she excused herself on the grounds that she wanted to go and get herself smartened up at the hairdresser, just in case this beautiful man by some lovely chance wasn't in love with his mother or the man who directed the series.

'Do people usually talk about him like that?' I asked Rita.

'About who?' she said.

'About Andy Sparks,' I said relentlessly.

'Oh, I suppose they do,' she said uncaringly. 'I mean he's quite famous really, isn't he? In everyone's homes every night – as they say.'

'Did you know him before he was a star?' I asked.

'No, I only got to know him a couple of years ago,' she said.

'Are you fond of each other?' I asked, again amazed at my bravery.

'Why?' she said.

'Well, I thought that he seemed very dependent on you the other night.'

'Oh, he was just pissed the other night,' she said.

There was a silence.

'Look,' I said. 'I don't want to talk about him if you don't. I just thought it was interesting, there you are knowing him very well while we just had to do bits and pieces about him to make up that feature. I suppose I wonder why you didn't say anything.'

'And have my picture in the paper you mean? Like Andy Sparks and the girl he can't have ... that sort of thing.'

'No, of course we wouldn't have done anything like ...'

'Of course you would,' she said flatly. 'You work on a newspaper.'

'There might have been a bit of pressure yes, but in the end it would have been up to you. Come on, Rita, you work with us, you're part of our team, we wouldn't rat on you that way.'

'Maybe,' she said.

'But why can't he have you ...?' I went on. 'You said Andy Sparks and the girl he can't have.'

'Oh well, I'm married to someone else,' she said.

'I see,' I said, though I didn't.

Another silence.

'And does he want to marry you, Andy, I mean?'

'Oh yes, I think Andrew would like to, but I don't think he really knows what he wants.'

'Do you not want to leave your husband?' I asked, remembering suddenly that there had been no sign of a man around that little flat.

'He's inside, served four years of fifteen, he'll probably have to do two more anyway.'

'Oh God, I'm sorry I asked.'

'No you're not, if you hadn't asked you wouldn't know. You want to know, it's partly you yourself, it's partly your job. You all like to know things.'

It was the longest speech I'd heard her make. I didn't know what to say.

She went on.

'Listen, I'm not coming back to the office. I don't want to go back now, because everyone already knows I know him. Oh yes they do, you told them, but you told them not to mention it, I'm not a fool. I can't bear offices where everyone knows everything about everyone else, that's why I stayed so long with you lot ... you didn't talk too much about your own lives, and you didn't pry into mine. I thought you'd like me being fairly buttoned up ... but no, it's all of you who've been doing the prying ...'

'I understand what you mean, Rita, honestly I do. The girls who did your job before were always so boring about their boyfriends and their life's history ... but seriously I understand if ...'

She looked at me.

'You understand nothing if I may say so. You don't understand the first little thing. And because it isn't clear to you at once, you turn it all into a little mystery and have to solve it. You don't understand why Andrew fancies me, you don't understand why I wait for a husband to come out of prison, you don't understand whether those kids Martie and Anna are mine or not.'

'It's none of my business,' I said, distressed and unable to cope with the articulate and very, very angry Rita. 'I can't say anything right now.'

44

Rita calmed down. Her eyes didn't flash, but they were not back to the dead dull look they normally held.

'Well, I could tell you a few things which would give you information, but you still wouldn't *understand*. Martie and Anna aren't my girls, they're Nat's. Nat is my husband. Nat is in gaol because he beat Myrtle to death. Myrtle was my best friend. Myrtle always loved Nat. Nat never loved Myrtle but he had two children by her. Even after he married me, he would see Myrtle. I knew, I didn't mind, that's the way Nat was. I knew it at the time, I know it now. Myrtle found this other fella, he wanted to marry her, take the kids and all he would. Myrtle told Nat, Nat said no, he didn't want another man raising his kids. Myrtle asked me what she should do. I said I thought she should marry the other fella, but then my advice was prejudiced.

'Myrtle said I was right, and she told Nat. They had a great row. Nat he lost his temper and he beat Myrtle and he beat her, and she died. I telephoned the police and they came, and they took him, and he got fifteen years and I look after Anna and Martie.'

She paused and took a drink of her wine, and though I didn't understand I could approach an understanding of how strong she must have been, must still be.

'And you won't understand either why Andrew wants me to go away with him. He just needs me. I don't know whether he loves me or not, or whether he knows what love is, but he needs me, because I . . . well I'm what he needs. And he doesn't understand either, he can't understand that Nat don't mind me seeing him. He knows that Nat has a lot of friends who tell him or his friends what's going on. But Nat doesn't mind me going about with a white man, a white actor from the television. Nat thinks that's just company for me. Now can you understand any of that at all?'

At the end of the week when the bird-brain's story appeared it was pretty tame stuff. She did have an angle that Andy Sparks had some mystery woman in his life, someone he leaned on, someone he needed, but was not prepared to discuss.

Rita came around that day to collect some things she'd left in the drawer of her desk, and to pick up her salary. She came at lunch-time when there was nobody there, except her replacement, who was full of chat and said that she had told Rita all about her fiancé being mean with money. She asked Rita if she thought that was a bad omen. Rita had said that she couldn't care less.

'Odd sort of woman, I thought,' said the replacement. 'Very untidy, sort of trampishly dressed really. Funny that she wasn't more pleasant. Black people are usually happy-looking, I always think.'

Queensway

Pat wished that she didn't have such a lively imagination when she was reading the advertisements. When she saw something like 'Third girl wanted for quiet flat. Own room, with central heating' she had dark fears that it might be a witches' coven looking for new recruits. Why mention that the flat was quiet? Could central heating be some code for bonfires? But she couldn't afford a flat of her own, and she didn't know anyone who wanted to share, so it was either this or stay for ever in the small hotel which was eating into her savings.

She dreaded going for the interview, which was why she kept putting off answering any of the offers. What would they ask her? Would they give her a test to see whether she was an interesting conversationalist? Might they want to know all about her family background? Did they ask things like her attitude towards promiscuity, or spiritualism, or the monarchy? Or would it be a very factual grilling, like could she prove that she wouldn't leave a ring around the bath or use the phone without paying for her calls?

There were about twenty women working in the bank, why did none of them want to share, she complained to herself. At least she knew something about them, that they were normal during the daytime anyway. But no, they were all well-established in London, married to men who wouldn't do the shopping, or living with blokes who wouldn't wash their own socks, or sharing flats with girls

47

who wouldn't clean up the kitchen after them. There was no place in any of their lives for Pat.

Three months was all she was going to allow herself in the hotel, three months to get over the break-up of her home, to calm herself down about Auntie Delia being taken away to hospital and not recognizing anyone ever again. It was better, the doctors said, that Pat should go right away, because Auntie Delia really didn't know who she was any more, and would never know. She wasn't unhappy, she was just, well there were many technical terms for it, but she was in a world of her own.

If you have worked in a bank in Leicester, you can usually get a job working in a bank in London. But if you've lived with Auntie Delia, funny, eccentric, fanciful, generous, undemanding, for years and years, it's not so easy to find a new home.

'What should I ask them?' she begged the small, tough Terry who knew everything, and who had no fears about anything in this life. 'I'll feel so stupid not knowing the kind of questions that they'll expect *me* to ask.'

Terry thought it was so simple that it hardly needed to be stated.

'Money, housework and privacy, are the only things girls fight about in flats,' she said knowledgeably.

'Find out exactly what your rent covers, make sure there aren't any hidden rates to be paid later, ask how they work the food – does everyone have their own shelf in the fridge, or do they take it in turns buying basics? If you are all going to have a week each in charge of the food, get a list of what people buy and how much they spend. Stupid to have you buying gorgeous fresh-ground coffee or expensive tea, when they only get instant and tea bags.'

'And what should I ask about housework?' Pat wondered.

'Do they have a Hoover, if so who uses it and when? It would be awful if they were all manic house cleaners, washing down paintwork every day. And examine the place carefully, they might be so careless that the place is full of mice and rats.'

Privacy meant that Pat was to inquire what arrangements they had about the sitting-room: did people book it if they were going to ask anyone in, or did everyone eat, play, watch telly together, or did people entertain in their own bedrooms?

So, armed with all this intelligence, she dialled the 'Third Girl wanted, lovely flat, near park, own room, friendly atmosphere' advertisement. Auntie Delia would have snorted at the ad, and said that they sounded like a bunch of dikes to her. Pat still couldn't believe that Auntie Delia didn't snort and say outrageous things any more.

The girl who answered the phone sounded a little breathless.

'I can't really talk now, the boss is like a devil today, he says I shouldn't have given this number. Can I have your number and I'll phone you back later when he leaves the office? It's a super flat, we wouldn't want to leave it in a million years, it's just that Nadia went off to Washington and we can't afford it just for two.'

Pat didn't like the sound of it. It seemed a bit fast and trendy. She didn't like people who said 'super' in that upward inflection, she didn't like the thought of people suddenly dashing off to Washington, it was too racy. And she thought the name Nadia was affected. Still, she might use them as a rehearsal. There was no law saying you had to take the first flat you saw.

The breathless girl rang back ten minutes later. 'He's gone out for an hour,' she confided. 'So I'm going to make use of it, ringing all the people back. I thought I'd start with you because you work in a bank, you might get us all an overdraft.'

Pat took this little pleasantry poorly, but still you had to practise flat-getting somewhere, and she arranged to call at eight o'clock. She made a list of questions, and she promised herself that she would take everything in, so that she would go better equipped to the next and more serious interview.

It was an old building, and there were a lot of stairs but no lift. Perhaps they all became permanently breathless from climbing those stairs. Feeling foolish to be feeling nervous, Pat rang the bell. It had a strange echoing chime, not a buzz. It would have, thought Pat. Nadias, and Washingtons, and Supers, naturally they'd have to have a bell that pealed, rather than one which buzzed.

Joy wasn't at all breathless now that she was home. She

49

wore a long housecoat, and she smelled of some very, very expensive perfume. She was welcoming, she remembered Pat's name, she apologized for the stairs but said that you got used to them after a month or so. There were eighty-three steps, counting the flat bits between floors, and they did encourage you not to be forgetful about things like keys.

Pat stared around the hall. It was literally covered in pictures and ornaments, and there were rugs on the walls as well. At one end there were a couple of flower baskets hanging and at the other a carved hall-stand full of dried flowers.

'It's far too nice to sit inside,' said Joy, and for a wild moment Pat thought that they would have to go down all the stairs again before she had even seen the flat.

'Come into Marigold's room, and we'll have a drink on the balcony.'

Marigold! thought Pat. Yes, it would have to be Marigold.

A big room, like one of those film-sets for an Anna Neagle movie, with little writing-desks, and a piano with photographs on top. There were flowers here too, and looped lacey curtains leading out to a balcony. There in a wheelchair sat Marigold. The most beautiful woman that Pat had ever seen. She had eyes so blue that they didn't really seem to be part of a human body. She could have played any number of parts as a ravishing visitor from Mars. She had so much curly hair, long, shiny and curly, that it looked like a wig for a heroine, but you knew it wasn't a wig. She smiled at Pat, as if all her life she had been waiting to meet her.

'I wish Joy would tell people I live in a wheelchair,' she said, waving at Pat to get her to sit down. She poured some white wine into a beautiful cut crystal glass and handed it to her. 'I honestly think it's so unfair to let people climb all those stairs and then face them with what they think will be a nursing job instead of a home.'

'Well I don't, I never, you mustn't . . .' stammered Pat.

'Rubbish,' said Joy casually. 'If I said you were in a wheelchair nobody would ever come at all. Anyone who has come, wants to move in, so I'm right and you're wrong.'

'Have you had many applicants?' asked Pat.

'Five, no six including the lady with the cats,' said Joy.

Pat's list had gone out of her head, and she had no intention of taking it from her handbag. They sat and talked about flowers, and how wonderful that in a city the size of London people still had a respect for their parks, and rarely stole plants or cut blooms for themselves from the common display. They talked on about the patchwork quilt that Marigold had made, how difficult it was to spot woodworm in some furniture, and how a dishonest dealer could treat it with something temporary and then it all came out only when you had the thing bought and installed. They had more wine, and said how nice it was to have an oasis like a balcony in a city of ten million or whatever it was, and wondered how did people live who didn't have a view over a park.

'We must have a little supper,' Marigold said. 'Pat must be starving.'

No protests were heeded, a quick move of her wrist, and the wheelchair was moving through the pots and shrubs of the balcony, the flowers and little writing bureaux of the bedroom, the bric-à-brac of the hall, and they were in a big pine kitchen. Barely had Joy laid the table for three before Marigold had made and cooked a cheese soufflé, a salad had been already prepared, and there was garlic bread, baking slowly in the oven. Pat felt guilty but hungry, and strangely happy. It was the first evening meal anywhere that seemed like home since they had taken Auntie Delia away.

She felt it would be crass to ask how much did people pay and who bought the groceries, and what kind of cleaning would the third girl be expected to do. Neither Marigold nor Joy seemed to think such things should be discussed, so they talked about plays they had seen, or in Marigold's case books she had read, and it was all as if they were just three friends having a nice dinner at home instead of people trying to organize a business deal.

At eleven o'clock Pat realized by the deep chiming of a clock that she had been there three hours. She would have to make a move. Never had she felt socially so ill at ease. She wondered what she should say to bring the visit to an end and the subject of why she was there at all into the open. She knew quite a lot about them. Marigold had polio and never left the flat. Joy worked in a solicitor's office as a clerk, but next year was going to go into apprenticeship there and become a solicitor too. Marigold seemed to have some money of her own, and did the housework and the cooking. They had met some years ago when Marigold had put an ad in the paper. Marigold had found the flat.

Nadia was mentioned, a little. There were references to Nadia's room and Nadia's clock, which was the big one that chimed, and some chat about the time they had made the curry for Nadia's dinner-party and everyone had gone on fire from it.

Resolutely Pat stood up and said that her little hotel closed at midnight and she had better get back, as they didn't have a night-porter.

'Well, when shall we expect you?' asked Marigold.

Pat, who hadn't even been shown her room, hadn't been informed about how much rent, what kind of lifestyle was to be expected, was stunned.

'What about the five other people, and the lady with the cats?' she asked desperately.

'Oh no,' said Marigold.

'No indeed,' said Joy.

'Well, can I think about it?' Pat asked, trying to buy time. 'I don't know whether I could afford to live here, and you mightn't like my friends, and we haven't really sorted anything out.'

Marigold looked like an old trusted friend who has suddenly and unexpectedly been rebuffed.

'Of course you must decide for yourself, and perhaps you have somewhere else in mind. We are terrible, Joy, not to give Pat details of rent and things. We're simply hopeless.'

'The rent is £20, and we usually spend about £10 a week each on food, and flowers and wine,' said Joy.

That was expensive, but not for what you got. You got a magnificent home, you got lovely meals, you got two very bright nice women to live with.

Pat heard her own voice saying, 'Fine. Yes, if you think I'd fit in here with you, that's fine. Can I come at the weekend?'

That night she wondered what she had done. Next morning she wondered whether she had been insane.

'I don't know,' said tough little Terry. 'If the food's as good as all that, if the one in the wheelchair does all the work, if the place is like something out of *Home and Garden*, I think you're laughing. If you don't like it you can always move out.'

'I didn't even look at my bedroom,' said Pat with a wail.

'They'll hardly give you a coal-hole,' said Terry practically.

Joy rang her breathlessly that day.

'It's super that you're coming. Marigold's so pleased. She asked me to tell you that there's plenty of room in your bed-sitting-room for anything you want to bring, so don't worry about space. Any pictures or furniture you like.'

Pat wondered why Marigold didn't ring herself. She was at home, she didn't have to avoid a spying boss. Pat also wondered whether this was a polite way of telling her that there were four walls and nothing else in her room.

On Saturday she arrived with two students who ran a flat-moving service. They carried up her little tables, her rocking-chair, and her suitcases. They had cluttered up her hotel bedroom ridiculously, and she wondered whether there would be any more room for them where she was going. As they all puffed up the eighty-three steps, Pat felt very foolish indeed.

Joy let them in, with little cries of excitement. They paraded through the bedecked hall to a huge sunny room, which had recesses for cupboards, a big bed and a wash-basin. Compared to the rest of the flat it looked like an empty warehouse.

Joy fussed along behind them. 'Marigold said we should empty it so that you wouldn't feel restricted. But there's lots of furniture available. There are curtains and shelves for these,' she waved at the recesses. 'Marigold thought you might want your own things.'

Pat paid the students, and sat down in the warehouse. Even her rocking-chair looked lost. When she unpacked it wouldn't be much better. Auntie Delia's things would look lovely here. All those monstrous vases, even that beaded curtain. Maybe she should send for them. They were all in the little house in Leicester. They would be hers when Auntie Delia died. Strictly speaking they were hers already, since she had rented the house out just to get money to pay for her poor Aunt in the nursing-home. The rent covered the fees. The tenants didn't like all the overcrowding from the furniture but Pat had insisted the house should remain untouched since Auntie Delia *could* get better one day and *might* come home. She felt slightly disloyal thinking about taking Auntie Delia's treasures, but surely she couldn't live in a barn like this, while Auntie Delia lived in a world of her own, and the tenants lived in a house that they thought vastly over-stuffed with things they didn't like.

It was morning coffee time, so she gathered from the smell of fresh coffee coming from the kitchen. She was right, they assembled on the balcony, and had coffee from lovely china cups.

'I'll be sending to Leicester for my real furniture this week,' she said.

'We'll be dying to see it,' said Marigold, her china-blue eyes lighting up with excitement.

'And I must give you some money and everything,' blurted out Pat. 'I'm not much good at this you know, not having shared a flat before.'

'Oh, Joy will look after that,' said Marigold. 'She's so good with money, working in that office, where there's a lot of accountancy. She should have been a solicitor from the start you know, it's so silly to have waited until she's twenty-seven before starting her indentures.'

'I'd never have done it at all if it weren't for you,' said Joy gratefully., 'I'd still be working on there and taking my money each week.'

'It would have been pointless,' said Marigold. Her blue eyes looked out over the park, where people who weren't in wheelchairs jumped and played and ran about.

Pat sighed happily. It was so peaceful here and she had the whole week-end before facing the bank again. Nobody ever told you how easy it was to find a flat.

'Would you like me to do any shopping or anything?' she asked helpfully.

'Joy does that on Friday nights, we're very well organized,' smiled Marigold. 'We have a small deep freeze as well. It helps a great deal.'

While the rest of London sweated and fussed and shopped and dragged themselves through traffic jams or in crowded trains to the seaside, Joy and Marigold and Pat sat peacefully reading, listening to music, or chatting. By Monday Pat felt she had been on a rest-cure. She and Joy had done a lot of the washing-up, and preparing of things, rougher jobs like peeling potatoes and cutting up meat, and taking out rubbish.

Joy was friendly and eager to do everything, Marigold was gentle, serene and calm. Pat began to think that she couldn't have found two more perfect flat-mates.

On Sunday night she telephoned the people in Leicester and asked them to arrange to have seventeen pieces of furniture, some huge, some tiny, collected and delivered to London.

Nobody had telephoned the flat, nobody had gone out. Pat wondered what happened if you invited a friend in for supper. Would they all eat as a foursome? She saw no other way.

She gave Joy £80, and asked what to do about the tenner for food.

'I'll spend £20 this week, and you spend it next week,' said Joy cheerfully.

Pat wondered where Marigold's tenner came into it but said nothing. Why upset things? Things are not always so peaceful in life, it's silly to question just for the sake of questioning.

On Tuesday she rang Joy at work to say that she was going to the theatre so would not be home for dinner.

'Oh.' Joy sounded upset.

'But that's all right, isn't it?' asked Pat. 'Marigold won't start to cook until we get home anyway, so it's not a question of letting her know in advance. I'd ring her at home but I . . . well, I just thought I'd ring you.'

'Oh yes, it's better to ring me,' said Joy. 'No, no problems. I'll pop home at lunch-time and tell her, it's not far. Don't worry.'

It all seemed very odd to Pat, but she put it out of her mind.

On Thursday her furniture arrived. Marigold was delighted with it. She whirled around in the wheelchair, stroking this and patting that.

'Lovely inlay,' she said.

'We must strip this down,' she said.

'What a magnificent curtain. Wouldn't it look lovely on the balcony?' she said.

So of course Pat, flattered and pleased, hung Auntie Delia's bead curtain up on the balcony, where indeed it looked lovely.

That night she asked if they ever heard from Nadia how she was enjoying Washington.

'No, we've not heard,' said Marigold.

'Nadia doesn't write many letters,' said Joy.

'What did she do, I mean what job had she?' asked Pat. Her slight jealousy of Nadia had disappeared, now she had only curiosity.

'She worked in an antique shop,' said Joy.

'Managed an antique shop,' said Marigold.

'Well, she worked there first,' laughed Joy. 'But Marigold told her she knew much more than anyone in it, and gave her confidence, so she ended up managing it for Mr Solomons.'

'She knew twice as much as Mr Solomons from the start,' said Marigold.

'Anyway Mr Solomons fancied her enormously, so that it didn't hurt,' said Joy with a giggle.

'Did she fancy him?' asked Pat with interest.

'Not until Marigold told her to have some intelligence and fancy him,' giggled Joy again.

'Oh,' said Pat.

Marigold seemed to think some clarification was called for.

'It always strikes me as silly to go to bed with half-drunk people, who forget it, or who feel embarrassed by it, or who do it so often that it's meaningless, and then refuse to go to bed with someone like Mr Solomons who would appreciate it, would remember it with affection, and would advance Nadia because of it. It just seems a foolish sort of thing to have a principle about.'

Put that way, thought Pat, it was unanswerable.

'But she left him all the same?' she probed.

'Oh no, she didn't leave Mr Solomons,' said Joy laughing. 'Mr Solomons left her. He had a heart attack and went to live in the country, so she managed his place for him, and took a share in the profits.'

'And had a very nice cut and first refusal on everything

they stocked,' said Marigold, stroking the little mahogany cabinet beside her, almost sensuously.

'So why Washington?' asked Pat.

'She's running a little antique shop in Georgetown now,' said Marigold distantly. 'Very different kind of stuff, I'm sure.'

'She got sort of unsettled, and took the first job she heard of,' said Joy artlessly.

'Some silly business with a chap who used to restore paintings, very silly really,' said Marigold. And the conversation about Nadia stopped there. It was as clear a break as if 'End of Episode One' had been written in fire in the air.

Out of sheer curiosity, Pat stopped in Solomons' antique shop. There was no elderly owner type about, so she supposed that the good proprietor's heart could not yet have recovered from Nadia's exertions.

She asked how much they would give her for Aunt Delia's inlaid cabinet if she were to sell it. She described it very carefully.

'About five hundred pounds,' said the young man. 'Depends on what condition it's in, of course, but not less I'd say.'

That was odd. Marigold had said it was pretty but without value. Marigold said she should take great care of it because it might be worth fifty pounds. Imagine Marigold not knowing how much it was worth. A flaw in the lovely, graceful, all-knowing Marigold. A flaw no less.

'Is Nadia still here?' she asked on impulse.

'No, why, you a friend of hers?' the man asked.

'No,' said Pat. 'I just know people who know her.'

'Oh, she left here a few weeks ago. Kevin would know where she is.' He pointed out a young and very attractive, bearded, bending figure, who was examining the frame of a picture.

'It doesn't matter really,' said Pat hastily, thinking this might be the silly young man of Marigold's description.

'Hey, Kevin, this lady's a friend of Nad's.'

Kevin stood up. He was very handsome in a definitely shabby, ungroomed way. Pat could see that his nails, his unwashed hair wouldn't have fitted into the elegant furniture back in the flat.

'I was just looking around, and I remembered that this is where the girl who lived in the flat where I've just moved in used to work . . .' said Pat apologetically.

'Have you moved in there?' asked Kevin flatly.

'Yes, a few days ago.'

'Have you moved all your stuff in?' he asked.

'Well yes, yes I have,' Pat's voice trailed away. She felt unreasonably frightened.

'Did she tell you it's worth buttons, peanuts?'

'No,' said Pat defensively. 'Marigold said it's very nice furniture and I must take care of it. Why, anyway?'

'Will you tell her you've been in here?' he asked very unemotionally.

'I might, I might not. Why do you ask?' said Pat. She was definitely frightened now, which was ridiculous. She also knew that she would never admit to Marigold that she had nosed around Nadia's old place of employment and nosed out Nadia's silly young man.

'I don't think you will,' he said. 'Nadia never told her anything towards the end, she was absolutely terrified of her. So was I. It's her eyes, they're not human.'

'They're just too blue,' said Pat. 'She can't help that.'

'No, but she can help a lot of things. Do you know that she hasn't polio at all?'

'I don't believe you,' said Pat, feeling her legs getting weak.

'No, she hasn't, that's why none of them ring her at home. She goes out, you know, when everyone's at work.'

'Don't be ridiculous.'

'No, I saw her several times running down the stairs, and taking a taxi. I took a photograph of her once to prove it to Nadia, but she said it was trick photography.'

'But she's paralysed,' said Pat.

'So she says. It's nice being paralysed if you get everyone else to do all the work, pay all the bills, and live in fear of you.'

'Don't you think that someone would have to be mad to pretend to have polio, just to get out of carrying out the rubbish?'

'Marigold is mad, very mad,' he said.

Pat sat down on a reproduction sofa.

'Didn't you guess?' he asked.

'I don't believe it,' said Pat.

'Nadia doesn't to this day,' said Kevin.

'Is that why she went to Washington?' asked Pat.

'She's not in Washington, she's back in my flat. In Clapham,' he said. 'She told them she was going to the States, that was the only reason that Marigold let her go.'

'You mean she has no job, and just lives in your flat because she's afraid of Marigold?' Pat said. 'I don't believe a word of it.'

'Go down there and see,' he said. 'She'll be sitting there complaining about the noise, and saying how little light there is, and how cramped the place seems to be. She doesn't even bother to get dressed properly, she hangs about all day complaining. That's what Marigold has done to her.'

'Does she want to be back in the flat?'

'She wants it so much I think she's becoming as mad as Marigold. "It was so peaceful. We were so gracious. We had such lovely music, not the neighbours' trannies." That's all she says, day in, day out.'

'Why did she leave it if she liked it so much?' asked Pat, almost afraid to hear the answer. Everything Nadia said about the flat was so true, there might be some truth in Kevin's whole terrible tale.

'She left it because I told her that she had given all her lovely furniture to this woman, that she had turned herself into a prostitute for her, that she had cut off her whole life for her, that she was working to support her. I told her to examine all these statements and if she thought they were true to move out. So she did and they were and she moved. But not without tissues of lies of course about Washington, which that nice silly Joy believed but Marigold saw through at once. Marigold didn't mind anyway, she had loads of stuff, hundreds of pounds worth, from Nad over the years, and she'll always get other slaves.'

'But Joy's normal.'

'She used to be, when she had a bit of a life of her own, and boyfriends, and big plates of spaghetti with the girls from work. She should have been married years ago and have three nice fat children by now, instead of trying to become a solicitor and earn more money for that Marigold.'

'You're very bitter about her.'

'I'm bleeding obsessed with her, that's what I am. She's ruined Nadia totally, she's turned Joy into a zombie, there was another one there too, I can't remember her name, but she had to go out to bloody Africa as a missionary or something to get over it all. Having left some very nice lamps and some very good old cut glass thank you.'

Pat's heart missed something of its regular movement. She remembered admiring the lamps, and Marigold had said they were from a dear friend who went to Africa and didn't need them.

It was the end of her lunch-hour. She walked out without saying anything. She knew where to find him if she needed to know any more. He would take her home to meet Nadia if she wanted confirmation of it all. She was a free, grown-up woman, nobody could keep her there against her will.

On the way back to the bank she passed an expensive flower shop. It had unusual little potted plants. One of them was very, very blue. It had a long name but Marigold would know it anyway. It would look lovely on the balcony table. It would be so peaceful there this evening after work. It was like a dream world really. It would be such a misery trying to get everything out of the flat now that she had just got it in. Anyway, why should she? Kevin was just a silly young man. Jealous obviously because Nadia had been so happy in the flat. Anyone would be happy in that flat, it was so very, very peaceful, you didn't need anyone else or anything else in the world.

Lancaster Gate

It was funny the way things turned out. If she hadn't made that huge scene, and cried, and nearly choked herself crying, and admitted all kinds of weaknesses, she wouldn't be here now. She would be back in the flat, cleaning the cooker, polishing the furniture, ironing his shirts, so that he would think it was wonderful to have all these home comforts and value her more.

She would have gone to the cinema maybe, but maybe not. Films were so full of other people's relationships, and she kept identifying, and saying 'If I behaved more like her, would he value me more?', or wondering why some screen woman could be so calm when everything was collapsing around her. Lisa could never be calm. She could pretend at calmness very successfully, but deep down it was churn, churn, churn. Sometimes she was surprised that he couldn't hear her heart sort of hitting against her bones, she could hear it thudding as well as feel it from inside, she could actually hear the wuff wuff sound it made. But fortunately he never managed to hear it, and she could always fool him into thinking she was relaxed and at ease. Sometimes the nights that had started with her heart thudding very seriously had turned out to be their best nights, because she acted out the calm role so well. Lisa had often thought how extraordinarily easy it was to fool someone you loved and who loved you.

Or who sort of loved you. But no, no, don't start that,

61

don't start analysing, worrying, your heart will begin the booming thing again, and you've got nothing to boom about. Here in London, staying in a big posh hotel, signing the room-service dockets with his name, putting the Mrs bit in casually as if you had been doing it for years and it was now second nature. She wondered how long it took married people to forget their single names. Brides were always giggling about it. She supposed it would take about three weeks, about the same time as it took you to remember each January that the year had changed and that you must write a different date.

And it was what they called a glorious day on the weather forecast, very flowery indeed for the Met Office, but that was the word the man had used, and she had run to the window to see if he was right, and he was. There were railings across the road and people were putting up pictures, and postcards, and souvenirs, to sell to the passing tourists. And they seemed to be shouting to each other and laughing. They must know each other from meeting every week-end here, and they didn't sound like rivals or enemies. They didn't look as if they'd mind if a passing tourist bought from one rather than another. They were unpacking little canvas stools as well, and some of them had flasks. They were old and young. Lisa thought it was a funny kind of life. She wouldn't be able for it, her old anxiety would show. People wouldn't buy from her because she would have an anxious face wanting them to buy, and the more they passed her by because of her anxious face the more anxious it would become. But then that was the same kind of vicious circle that everyone kept getting caught in. It was like the whole problem with Him. If she felt unsure of him and thought that he was losing interest in her, she became strained and worried and not the carefree girl he had once fancied, and so he *did* start to lose interest, and because she could see this happening she became more strained and worried, and he lost more interest.

But stop, stop. Not today, today is glorious. It has been defined as such by the weatherman on the radio, than whom there must be surely no saner, soberer judge. And today you don't need to act at being relaxed, you are. He's there in the bathroom shaving, he's happy, he's glad you're here. You've made love a half an hour ago, he liked it, he's humming to himself. You make him happy or happier than he'd be if you weren't here. You're fine really. Remember that. He didn't have to take you with him to London for the conference, now did he? He couldn't have been planning something else, something awful like meeting someone else, if he took you so readily.

Lisa smiled happily, thinking of how readily he had agreed to take her with him. She hadn't meant to ask at all. She had packed his case yesterday morning ... was it only yesterday? Friday, it must have been. She had been polishing his shoes.

'You don't need to do that,' he had said, a bit embarrassed.

'I was doing my own,' she had lied.

'They're suede, funny face,' he had said, laughing.

What was it? It couldn't have been funny face, he called her that a lot, it was meaningless as an endearment, it wasn't even special. He called his daughter funny face on the phone ... often. He called his secretary funny face. Once she had been holding for him on the phone, and she could hear his voice clearly as he crossed the office. 'Get me a cup of coffee, funny face,' he had said. 'I've got a bugger of a day.' It was probably because he knew she wore suede shoes. Idiotic, it couldn't have been that. Put baldly it was really madness. What was it then? Why did two tears fall down onto the shining leather shoes in her hand? She could have hit herself with rage. It wasn't as if she knew it was going to happen. You always sort of know when you're going to cry but not this time. It was automatic, as if someone had tinkered about with her tear-ducts when she wasn't looking. And once started there was no stopping. She dropped the shoes and said a hundred times that she was sorry, she didn't know what was wrong. She tried to laugh through this appalling shower of tears, and that made her worse. She would sort of catch her breath and cough, and then it would get worse, and there were actual whoops coming out of her at one stage.

He was astounded. He thought he was to blame.

'What did I say, what have I done?' he had said over and over. 'You knew I was going away today, you *knew*,' he had repeated. He felt cornered, he felt she was blaming him. She couldn't even stop this terrible heaving to assure him that of course she knew, and that today wasn't any worse than any other day. He looked very wounded.

'The conference starts on Monday. I want to get into top form for it, I don't want to arrive exhausted. I want to be there and rested, and to have made my own tour of the hotel. I don't want to be thought of as your typical Northern hick who arrives all impressed by everything. It's important, Lisa. You said you understood.'

The use of her name maybe. She stopped for a moment. She actually had breath to speak. But instead of saying what she meant to, something like *of course* she understood, she heard her own voice betraying her, ratting on her. She actually said, '*Why* do you have to go away? We could have had this week-end together, just the two of us. Nobody would have known we were here, it would have been lovely.'

When the words were said, she decided that she had now lost everything, that the whole hard uphill race had been lost. She didn't know to whom she had lost, but she had lost. He couldn't stand people who begged, people who made demands. He had told her that was why he had left his wife, why the great love of his life (which had not been his marriage) had ended, because these women made demands. They wanted more of him than he could give, they saw something wonderful in a forced intimacy, they thought that the phrase 'just the two of us' was safe and reassuring. He thought it was threatening and claustrophobic.

And because Lisa had thought that she had lost him, she abandoned herself to the tide. It was a great luxury, like getting into a warm bath when you're tired and cold. She had said all the unsayable things, the whines, the moans, the loneliness, how hard it had all been on her. How she had given him, if not the best years, then all the fun hours of her life, and for what? Nobody could know they lived together. Nobody could see them out together. It was clandestine and anxious-making, and leading nowhere, and she, Lisa, who was free, was abandoning every other man, every other chance of happiness, and for what? For someone who didn't give two damns about her. Well all right, it was all right. She kept repeating the words 'all right' as if they were a magic charm. She had no idea what she meant by them, but they were safer and less final than saying something even more hackneyed like 'it's all over'.

. He hadn't seemed relieved that it was all over or all right or whatever she meant; he hadn't seemed distressed, either. He looked interested, like he would have been interested in a farmer telling him about spraying crops, or a news-vendor explaining what margin of profit there was in selling papers. He sounded as if he might like to hear more.

'Come with me then,' he said.

He had never taken her anywhere before, it was too dangerous. He had always said that in his position he couldn't afford anyone to point at him about anything. Times were too tricky, things were too rough. He couldn't mean it now, he was just saying it to placate her, he knew she'd refuse for his sake. It was another ploy, another bluff. He had once explained to her why he won so much at poker. She had realized even then that the same rules that he used at the card-table he used everywhere.

As suddenly as he had asked her she accepted.

'Fine,' she said. 'I will. Where shall I meet you?'

No back-tracking, no well-perhaps-not-this-time. He was on as well, that was one of the rules of the game. If you offer, you must follow through.

'Nowhere near the office, too likely to be seen. Take a bus to the big petrol station on the London road. I'll meet you there at . . . ten past four.'

'Right,' she said. He kissed her and said it would be great, he'd like showing her London.

'You hardly know it any better than I do,' she said.

No tears, no joy, no excitement, no gratitude. He looked at her approvingly. It was almost as if he thought she had gained a few houspoints. She had faked grief, she had got him to take her to London. Well done Lisa. He said jaunt-ily that he wouldn't wait a minute after a quarter past four, and she said equally lightly that that was fine, and he left, suitcase in his hand, and she heard the car starting as he went off to work and to talk to the office funny face.

Lisa had felt light-headed, like the time she once went out in a speedboat, and nothing had been real. She sat down to steady herself. She must make a list. Obviously she wouldn't go to work. So what excuse this time? She didn't know how long she'd stay with him in London. The conference lasted four days, Monday to Thursday. She'd have to invent something that would take a week. Quick, she'd have to telephone in the next few minutes and alert the Head's secretary, before Assembly began and someone started looking for her. A death. Exactly, a death in London. Better than flu, a woman's disease, or a heavy cold. She dialled, she spoke, she waved her hands around in the air as she told the weary Miss Weston, the Head's tame dog, that an aunt, her nearest relative, was dying. She even got a bit sad about it as she filled in the form and details of this mythical aunt. No, there simply was nobody else, nobody at all, she had to go. She'd ring from London next week to tell them what was happening. She knew how terrible it would be trying to find a substitute at this late stage, but she had heard only just now, this minute, and she was going to London this afternoon. 'At ten past four,' she said meaninglessly but to make it more real in her own mind. Miss Weston said she would tell the Head, and implied that the job of telling the Head was far worse than saying good-bye to a favourite aunt. Miss Weston was never very good with small chat anyway.

Now, on with the list. Lisa had to get a smart case, she only had an old grip, not suitable at all, and what else? Take money out of the bank, get her hair done, ring her brother to make sure he didn't call her at school. He hadn't telephoned her for four months, but there was always the chance. Her brother was in his usual bad humour.

'You got me away from my scrambled eggs, they'll be all hard. Oh all right. No, of course I wouldn't telephone you, why should I? Oh very well. I don't know what you think you're doing. Have you read about the unemployment in this country? Where do you think you're going to get another job if you're fired? Sometimes I think you've no sense of responsibility. No, of course I won't say anything to anybody, but Lisa, I wish you'd tell me what you're up to. I was saying to Angela the other night that you are so secretive and you just ring me out of the blue to say the oddest kind of things. No, why the hell should I wish you a good time? I'm not able to run out on everything and everybody and dash off to London on some whim. Goodbye now, good-bye.'

No other friends to alert really. Funny after all the years

of living in the same town. But she'd see Maggie at lunch and she'd tell her, and they'd have a bit of a giggle, and then Maggie would say, 'Make sure he pays for you, I think he's mean,' and Lisa would defend him to the hilt, he wasn't mean, he was careful with money, and that's how he got where he was and had all the things he had. She admired him for it.

It was a rush but it was a great day. There had been a few valleys. Maggie said she had heard that his wife was expecting another baby. Lisa said that it couldn't be true, he hadn't even seen his wife for six months. Maggie said it took nine months to produce a baby and this one was nearly ready to be produced. Lisa said it was all ridiculous, he'd have told her, and Maggie said sure, and anybody would tell you it didn't have to be *his* baby just because it was hers, and Lisa brightened. She darkened a bit at the bank when she tried to take out £60 from her deposit account and the clerk told her she had only £50 in it. She was sure there was over £200, but of course things like avocados were more expensive than the things she ate when she lived alone, and she did buy lots of little things for the flat.

She bought him a Johnny Cash cassette that they could play in the car, the kind of music he liked. It was a new one, they assured her. She was there at 3.30 and by four o'clock she knew every car accessory that they make these days. She bought a chamois so that the assistant wouldn't think she was loitering with intent. At five past four she got a horrible feeling that he might have been joking. She really should have rung him to make sure he meant it, but that would have looked humble and she didn't want that. Suppose she saw his car flying past. Suppose just suppose he did stop there for petrol and saw her, and hadn't meant to take her. That wouldn't be merely humble, it would be pathetic. Lisa shook herself, physically, like a dog trying to get rid of drops of rain, but she was trying to get rid of these hauntings and fancies. She seemed to have them these days the way people got mosquito bites, or dandruff. And then she saw him pulling in and looking around for her.

And the four hours, well it had been like a dream sequence in a movie. Or rather, like one of those sequences where they show you people making a long journey across America, and they cut from shots of the car on one motorway to another, lights from petrol stations and hotels flash on and off, signposts to cities pass by – and they were in London, and they hadn't talked much, just sat beside each other listening to both sides of the Johnny Cash over and over, and Lisa never asked where they'd be staying or how they'd hide from all the people from his company who were bound to be at the hotel, or what day she was going to be sent home. She didn't want to break the magic.

And when they came to London he looked a bit helpless because he didn't know which way to go, and he turned right once when there was no right turn and a taximan shouted at him, and Lisa was secretly delighted because he looked vulnerable then, and like a little boy, and she wanted to hug him to take the shame away, but she made no move, and finally after an hour of going backward and forward he found the hotel and suddenly he was his old self again. Because the world of hotels is pretty much the same everywhere, it's just London traffic that can throw you.

She had wondered what to do about a wedding-ring. He had never bought her any kind of ring, and she hadn't liked to get one this morning when she was shopping . . . well, in case he thought she was being small-townish about it all. Perhaps people didn't wear rings when checking in, perhaps it was more sophisticated not to. She had worn gloves anyway, it seemed a good way of avoiding doing the wrong thing.

The foyer was huge and impersonal, but full of people and shops, and newspaper-kiosks and theatre booking-stands. It was very different from the hotel that she and Bill had stayed in when mother was ill, and had suddenly been taken into hospital in London. That time they stayed in a small hotel near the station, and the woman who ran it asked them for the money in advance, and Bill had said they would have to sleep in the same room to save paying for two. And the woman who ran the hotel had turned out to be nice and kind when she discovered that their mother was dying, and had made tea for Lisa, and had told her how her own mother had died.

And it was different from the hotel that they had all

stayed in when mother and father and Bill and herself had come to London for a week one October as a treat. That had been owned by a friend of father's, a North Country-man, and father said they wouldn't be robbed there like they would everywhere else. And it had been a vaguely unsatisfactory holiday for no reason that any of them ever understood and none of them ever dared say. Just a lot less than they all had hoped for probably.

But here in Lancaster Gate it was a different world and a different life, and he looked pleased that she was there and that was all that mattered. She smiled at him as the porter took their cases. She had bought one very like his, and got a cosy warm feeling in the lift because the cases looked like matching luggage, the kind of thing they might have been given as a wedding-present if they had been a normal couple.

And he must have ordered a room with a double-bed specially because she saw from the brochure she had been looking at in the lobby that most of the rooms had twin beds. And he gave her a kiss when the porter had gone, and said, 'There's nothing like a life of sin. Let's ring for a gin-and-tonic and let's go to bed.'

And they did, and then they went out to a restaurant where the Italian waiter asked them if they were married and Lisa said 'No' very quickly so that he wouldn't think she was trying to pretend in any way (except to the hotel) that she *was* his wife, and the waiter said he thought not, they looked too happy and too much in love. And Lisa's heart which hadn't pounded or thudded since that morning went into a little cotton-wool ball of happiness.

So it was indeed funny the way things turned out, she thought again. Instead of losing out by behaving like a weak wife-type, clinging, dependent, she was being patted on the back and taken on a nice happy trip to London. There was a knock at the door and she leaped off the bed to answer it, thinking it was breakfast. It wasn't, it was a bowl of fruit and some flowers with a Compliments card. She gave the boy twenty pence and hoped that it was enough. He came out of the bathroom, all clean and young-looking, a towel around his waist. He was as excited as a child and nearly as excited as she was.

'Who's it from, who's it from?' she begged.

He tried to look casual. 'I always arrange little surprises like this for you,' he said, teasing her, and they opened the card.

It was from the President of the Company, an American gesture, he said, to make the employees feel they are part of a happy family, to make them pull harder because they think they are being looked after. He was very pleased, even though he wouldn't show it.

'Must have taken a secretary a long time to write out all these personal cards,' he said, not wishing her to think that he thought the President had written it.

'Still,' said Lisa. 'They did go to the trouble.'

She reached out for the card, and her heart became a big ball of putty and sank down in her body. It was addressed to 'Mr and Mrs' and hoped that they would both enjoy their stay.

'Is it . . . is it to tell you that they *know* you've brought a woman with you?' she asked fearfully.

He looked unconcerned. Not at all, the secretary had probably found out from the hotel which delegates had checked in with their wives and put Mr and Mrs on those cards. Just administration. He was putting on the cuff-links she had given him and he gave her a kiss on the nose.

She felt that the day was a bit less glorious and immediately felt very angry with herself for feeling that way. What had happened? Nothing. She was a cheat and a tramp, and a mistress, and illegally registered in the hotel as the 'Mrs' she wasn't. But that was all rubbish. The first night she had gone to bed with him she had rid her mind of all those labels, they didn't count in anybody's mind except the fevered minds of a long-gone generation. Why was a silly card upsetting her?

The breakfast arrived and they sat by the window reading the two newspapers that had been sent up as well. She touched his hand when she poured him more coffee. He smiled, and she hoped in a beaten sort of way that it was going to be fairly glorious anyway.

'What shall we do?' he said.

'I'd like to look at the pictures and things they're hanging up on the railings down there. Maybe I might buy a couple of things.'

'It's bound to be rubbish,' he said, not disagreeably, but as one who knew about such things.

'All the same, it would be nice to stroll around and then maybe go for a walk in the Park,' she said.

'Perhaps we should move further away from the hotel,' he said. He was right, of course. It would have been idiocy to have hidden it for seventeen months back home, where such things were hard to hide, and then blow it in a city of ten million people, just by parading around in front of people who were bound to know him, and to know that she oughtn't to be there. Lisa agreed quickly.

'We can go anywhere else,' he said helpfully.

'We could get the underground to St Paul's and have a look at that,' she said eagerly, to show that she didn't mind being a second-best woman, a person who had to be hidden rather than paraded.

'Yes, we could do that,' he said.

'Or walk up to Oxford Street maybe, and look at the shops.'

'They'll be a bit crowded, Saturday morning,' he said.

She felt the familiar terror, the well-known realization that she was losing his interest came flooding over her. You counter that with brilliant acting, she told herself smartly. You don't give in, you don't allow yourself to look beaten or sulky. You act.

'Listen my love, I'm doing all the suggesting, I don't mind *what* we do. It's a glorious day, even the man on the wireless said so. I'll do whatever you'd like, or anyway I'll discuss it.'

She smiled the bright bird-like smile that she felt must look so phoney. She always thought she must look like a model in an advertisement on telly who has suddenly been told she must act.

But no, as always, he responded as he would have done to a normal remark.

'Well, I'll tell you what I'd *like* to do,' he said.

'Yes?' Mask set, eyebrows raised, mouth in inquiring smile.

'It sounds a bit odd but, well, I've arranged to have one of these executive health check-ups. You know, we were talking about them. They have them on Saturday mornings. Do everything: heart, blood pressure, X-rays, blood

71

tests, the lot. It makes more sense than spending hours and days at home.

'They have them on Saturdays so that executives can go without telling anyone at work what they're up to. When I thought I was going to be here by myself, I booked one for today, and sent a deposit. I could cancel it but you ... you know, it seems a pity. It would set my mind at rest.'

The fluttering fear that was never too far from her heart came back and buzzed at her, it even got into her eyes.

'Stop looking worried, funny face,' he said, laughing. 'Nothing happens to me, it's because I do things like this that I'm so healthy. They won't find anything wrong. It's just wise to have it done at forty-five, that's all.'

She was ten years younger and a hundred times slower in every way, in thinking, in walking, in making up her mind, in knowing what to say.

'Are you sure you don't have any pains or anything?' she faltered.

He was sure, and he was quite willing to cancel it. It was just that they didn't have anything like this at home, and you know that once you went for any kind of check-up back there, everyone knew about it, and they all had you buried before you came out of the doctor's surgery. Still, it did seem a pity to waste the nice morning, and she had been saying only yesterday that they didn't have much time together, just the two of them. Perhaps he would ring and cancel it.

She knew she was being manipulated when she insisted that he go. She knew he used the phrase 'just the two of us' in heavy inverted commas. She knew that he had never intended to back out of it for a minute. Anyway she thought it was a good idea for him to have the check-up. So it was on with the act.

No, nonsense, she would be very happy to stroll around herself. She'd meet him afterwards. She'd go down and look at those pictures that he didn't want to see. It was ideal really, they could each do what they wanted, and then meet for lunch.

He didn't know whether it would be over by lunch-time. But she thought that this was the point, that the check-up only took a couple of hours. Yes, well he hoped so but maybe they had better not make a firm arrangement for lunch just in case.

Oh act, act. Fine, that suited her too. After she had looked at the paintings on the railings, she'd have a quick look at Oxford Street, and then take the tube to St Paul's. She hadn't been there since she was a child, she'd love to see it again. Don't cling, don't cling, you mustn't appear dependent. Choose some very late time and he'll suggest earlier. He'll like you for saying you can manage alone, you'll like it if he says he wants you earlier. Don't ruin it, don't balls up the glorious day.

'Why don't we say six o'clock here!' Bright, light tone, utterly non-clinging, utterly ridiculous as a suggestion. His examination couldn't possibly take from eleven in the morning until six at night.

'That sounds about right,' he said, and the day went dark, but the voice stayed bright, and there were no give-away signs as she bounced cheerfully out the door.

The lobby looked less glittering and glamorous and Lon-donish. It looked big and full of people who trusted other people or didn't give a damn about other people. She looked at the house-phones on the wall. Should she ring up and just say 'Love you'? They did that to each other, or they used to a lot in the beginning. No, it was silly, there was nothing to be gained and it might irritate him. Why risk it?

She wound her way across the road, jumping this way and that to avoid the traffic, because it looked too far to walk to the pedestrian crossing, and anyway she was anxious to get to the other side. It reminded her of Paris, and all those thousands of water-colours of Notre-Dame, all of them exactly the same and all of them different prices, or so it seemed.

There was a young man with very red hair and a very white face looking at her.

'Scarf, lady?' he asked hopefully.

'I want to look at everything before I buy,' she said happily.

'Surprising more of you Northerners aren't killed if that's the way you cross roads up there,' he said good-naturedly.

He meant it nicely. It was to keep her chatting, she

knew that. She also thought that he fancied the look of her, which was nice. She felt it was so long now since anyone had fancied her that she wouldn't know how to react. But somehow his marking her out as a Northerner annoyed her, she was irritated, even though she knew it was said in friendship. Did she sound provincial, did she look provincial, crossing the road like that?

Suddenly she thought with a violence that made her nearly keel over, that there was a great possibility that he thought she was provincial too. That could be the reason why he wasn't prepared to make any public announcement of their being together. Not announcement, she didn't really want as much as that, she wanted . . . a bit of openness. It was bloody obvious now that she thought of it. Living with someone, having it off with someone, having an affair, all this was accepted now . . . by everyone.

She stood there, not even seeing the blur of Towers of London, Trafalgar Squares, and Beefeaters that waved like flags from the scarf-rack. She could only see her herself years ago at supper-time, listening to her mother talking about people who gave themselves airs. Her mother had wanted Lisa always to remember that she came from good stock. They could hold their heads up with any of them, they were as good as anyone for miles around, they had nothing hidden away that could never be dragged out. Lisa and Bill never knew what brought on these kind of statements, they had never even known what she was talking about. Suddenly Lisa knew. It was the reassurance game, it was trying to say 'it's all right'.

Lisa felt like shouting it out aloud this very moment. She had an urge to tell the boy with the red hair that her father had been a local government official, that her mother had been a nurse, that her mother's father had owned a chemist's shop. She wanted to say it in a voice so clear and loud that he would hear it, before he left for his check-up, so that he would realize how lucky he was to have got a girl from such good stock, who was so willing to play along in a shabby game with him. That it was against her training, her background, her . . . well her kind of people. She wanted him to know, without having to spell it out, that she was better than he was, better in the way that older people valued things, that she had come from respectable

74

people. His father had worked in the Potteries, that much she knew and only that.

Of course he had married into money, and why shouldn't he, a bright boy like him? Any family would have been delighted to have him as a son-in-law. Would her own family have liked him? Yes, her father would have admired him, her mother would have been a bit boringly embarrassing about stock, but she would have accepted him. However, she'd have liked him to know, if only there were some way of telling him indirectly, that her family wouldn't have fallen over themselves in gratitude ... that he'd have had to make an effort to be accepted.

Lisa's head cleared and she looked at the boy again.

'I don't feel very well,' she said, feeling she owed him some explanation of why she was standing there looking at him wildly.

'Do you want to sit down, darling?' he asked kindly, and pushed out a stool for her. He looked a bit worried and even embarrassed. His customer had turned out to be a nutcase. That's what he must be thinking, Lisa told herself miserably.

He gave her a cup of very sweet coffee from his little orange flask. Over the rim of the cup she looked up at the hotel. Was there any chance that he would be looking out the window and would see her sitting down, drinking coffee there? Would he be worried, would he rush down to know if she felt faint? What would she say if he did? But as the hot sweet coffee went down inside her chest, Lisa had another feeling too. No, he wouldn't be looking out the window, straining for a view of her crossing the road. *She* did that kind of thing, he didn't. She was the one who would look hopefully out the window of the flat at home to see him turning the corner in the evenings. If she was the late one home, he was always reading or looking at television. He never stood at windows. He wouldn't be looking down.

'I feel much better, thank you ever so much,' she said to the red-haired boy.

'You still look a bit shaky, love,' he said.

'Could I sit here for a little bit?' asked Lisa, more to please him really than because she wanted to. She thought he would like to feel he was doing her a service. She was right, he was delighted. He moved the stool back against the

75

railings and lit her a cigarette, while he talked to two Americans and sold them a wall-hanging with Big Ben on it.

'When they get home they'll probably have forgotten what city Big Ben is in,' he said. He didn't think much of Americans, he told her. Scandinavians were educated people, Americans weren't. He asked her if she was going to be in London for long.

'My husband is going to Harley Street for a check-up today,' she said cosily. 'It may depend on what he's told. But I think we'll be here a week.'

She wondered whether she was going mad, actually mad, at the age of 35. It did happen to people, they started telling the most fantastic, unreal tales and nobody noticed for a while, then they had to go and have treatment.

'Harley Street today, a Saturday?' said the red-haired boy cheerfully. 'Meeting some bird more likely. You won't find any doctors in Harley Street today. You'd better keep an eye on your old man, my darling, he's with some blonde.'

He smiled a big cockney grin, full of quickness and good humour. He liked most people he met, this boy did. He didn't particularly fancy her probably, he was like this with old dears of a hundred and with fellows as well.

'It's possible,' she said. 'Quite possible.'

The red-haired boy looked alarmed. She must look as if she were going mad again; he must be regretting his little pleasantry.

'He'd be mad if he was,' he said. 'Lovely woman like you, no blonde could be any better. No, he'd need his head examined he would, if he told you he was going to a doctor and went off to hold hands in a park with a blonde.'

His face had a kind of transparency about it. It was watery somehow, with pale eyes set far apart from each other. It was a very simple face. It wouldn't disguise things, and look differently to the way it was feeling. It wasn't the kind of face that could smile and tell you that its health needed a check-up if it wasn't true. That face could never become troubled and talk about its marriage having been a sad sort of thing, better not spoken of, if in fact his wife were pregnant and it were planning to try and get the marriage revved up again.

'Are you married?' she asked him.

'No darling, never met a lady that was worthy of me,' he said.

'Neither am I,' she said.

She didn't care what he thought. She tried not to look at the flicker of puzzlement and irritation that came over his white, transparent face. It was because of his face that she had decided to tell him the truth, even though it would have been better in the short encounter between them if she hadn't.

She got up, folded the stool together, and placed it very precisely beside the railings.

'I really do feel a lot better, thank you. I might come back and buy something from you later on,' she said.

'You do that, my darling,' he said, relieved that she was going. She felt that even here she had stayed too long, talked too much, revealed a dependence. Was she ever going to be able to stop?

There was an opening into the park and she walked in. The grass was yellowish, there hadn't been any rain for a long time. A series of glorious days probably. She looked at the people. No delegates to the conference, nobody from back home had arrived yet; there was no danger of being seen by anyone. And even though he was careful about his health, it was funny that he hadn't said anything about the check-up before. And why had they got a 'Mr and Mrs' card with the fruit and flowers? He must have said all along that he was bringing his wife with him. And the room had already had a double-bed in it, before he had planned for her to accompany him. And what kind of fool did he think she was to believe he was having an executive check-up all bloody day? Or did he care what she thought? Was it just a case of it being more comfortable to have an undemanding fool of a woman who paid her own way and wasn't any extra trouble than not to have one, or to leave her at home sulking?

She strolled around idly, noticing that everyone in the park seemed to be with other people. There were groups of girls, and there were families, and there were a lot of pregnant women walking with that proud waddle they develop, hands folded oddly over the bulk in front, managing to look

77

frail as well as huge, so that husbands had protective arms around shoulders.

And she wondered, did he have his real wife in London for the week-end, and was he in fact going to go back to her, and was it she who was pregnant or someone else? Maggie would say anything to get her nice friend Lisa out of this thing. Or did he have some other girl, who also had to be fobbed off with lies and hurried telephone calls? She knew how real his excuses could sound. She wondered whether any other woman in the whole world would have gone to live with a man who was not divorced and who went home every six months to see his daughter, but apparently didn't talk to his wife except about business matters.

She wondered if it was worth going back to the hotel to pick up the case. She thought not, really. It had cost £12 and that was a pity, but what was £12 compared to other things she had spent? She had her handbag with her and her money, there weren't many clothes at the hotel. She hadn't brought much with her in order not to appear too eager, not to look as if she was assuming that she was staying for the whole week.

She didn't make any plans about what was his and what was hers in the flat. She'd sort that out tomorrow or the day after when she got back, and she'd take what she felt like taking. She wouldn't take lots out of viciousness, or too little out of martyrdom.

She didn't even start fussing and worrying about what stations the trains went from and how to get there, or what times they were at, and how much they cost. She didn't even know whether she would go in to work on Monday and say her aunt hadn't died in London after all. It was strange, but she didn't even seem to be imagining how he would react when he came back at six o'clock and she didn't turn up. Would he contact the police? Would it embarrass him with the hotel and with everybody? Would he think she was dead? It didn't matter.

She always thought that things ended suddenly, that people had a big row, or they parted with clenched teeth and noble smiles like they did in old movies. And she stood still beside a seat which had a lot of old people sitting on it, and she took some deep breaths one after another as if she was testing to see how her heart was feeling, whether it was thudding, or if it was surrounded by that awful, horrible, empty feeling of fear like it so often was, when she thought he was angry or bored with her. And funnily it didn't seem to be in a bad state at all.

She wished she had someone to tell, someone who would congratulate her, someone who would be interested. If mother was alive . . . no, of course she couldn't have told mother about it, what was she dreaming about? Mother had been interested certainly, but you didn't tell mother about having affairs, that wasn't something people from our stock did, people who were busy holding their heads up with the best of them. And father, he might have liked the story if it had been about someone else. He used to listen to her tales about other people, and say, 'Fancy, aren't folk strange?' Maggie would treat it lightly, and probably come out with new stories about him, things she hadn't liked to tell Lisa at the time. And there was nobody in the staff-room she could tell, and Bill, well Bill and Angela would just have one of their worried conversations about her. She really had very few friends.

And that was the one cloud on her new freedom, she realized. That's what she'd miss, having him for a friend. In a few ways and some of the time, he had at least been a friend.

Marble Arch

These days she felt that the flower sellers, the men with piles of things that had fallen off lorries, the policemen and the road-sweepers were her friends. She felt they were all part of some kind of club, the only remaining English people in a sea of foreigners. It was a racist kind of thought perhaps, she said to herself, because if you started noticing how many people there were who smelled of garlic, or who wore face-veils, or head-dresses, then the next step might be to wish they weren't there. It would be better not to notice differences at all, to think that everything which walked on two feet was a fellow human.

Anyway she had no right to be anything but grateful to all the tourists. She reminded herself of this as an Arab thrust a piece of paper at her with an address down the Edgware Road on it, and she pointed him in the right direction. He was going to a chemist's shop, she noticed. She wondered whether it was for a prescription or to buy boxes of soaps and talcums. Without the Arabs her own business would have folded long ago. She sold handmade handbags in a shop within a shop. They were quite expensive. Young Londoners didn't have the money young Kuwaitis did.

Sophie unlocked her little shop and started to hang up the bags. She then got a stool and sat out in the morning sunlight waiting for custom. It was much more expensive to have a street frontage, but it trebled business. She was glad she had such a good head for business. She really needed it because nobody around her seemed to understand the first principles of earning a living. She frowned with the beginnings of a headache, and moved out of the sun. It had been a very late night.

It hadn't been night when she finally got to bed, it had been four o'clock in the morning. Eddie had brushed the hair out of his eyes and half-raised himself on an elbow as she left, but he was now back in a deep innocent sleep again and here she was sitting with a headache, trying to trap the tourists who came to Marble Arch, trying to keep awake and make a living for Eddie and herself.

She never thought of herself as earning a living for both of them. That wasn't the way the words or the ideas fell together. Only sometimes, when she had a headache or when they had talked long and without direction during the night, did she think wistfully how nice it would be if he was the one who got up in the mornings, and she was the one who could raise herself on an elbow and say 'Goodbye love, take it easy'. But that wasn't really considering an alternative, it was only thinking about things that would never be, like the way you sometimes imagined what it would be like to be a seagull when you saw one swooping backwards and forwards over a harbour.

Sophie thought a bit about last night's discussion. It hadn't been any different from the ones that had gone before, just longer. Eddie's dark brown eyes and their long black lashes looked dull with the pain of the world. They had lost all the flash and brilliance they had when he wasn't talking about the cruelty of the world. Dead they sat on his face as he spoke on bitterly about the producers who were pansies, the agents who were fairies, the script-editors who promised the moon, the misguided advice of friends who said, 'Well, why don't you just *go* to Framlingham or Fraserburgh or some ridiculous place and see what happens?'

Eddie wasn't going to just go anywhere. At thirty-seven he was too old now to just go to a stupid group of over-excited students or experimentalists and help them out with their productions. He had been in acting too long, learned too much, was too professional to give in, to sell the past. What had all these years been for if he was going to give in now? What would his love for Sophie mean if he was to allow that painted Jeffrey to feel him up and take him to that queers' pub as a possession, just in order that Eddie could get a part? No, life was cruel, and rotten, and the good people always lost out, and it was a plot, and you couldn't fight the system hoping to win, but at least you could try.

Sophie had never seen life as being cruel and rotten before she met Eddie, but she had always seen it as fairly difficult and tiring. She thought if you worked hard you made money, and then you had leisure time and you enjoyed that. If you were very lucky indeed you worked at something that wasn't awful, and then you enjoyed both work and leisure. She thought it must be very strange and sad to work in a world where there seemed to be steaming clouds of sexual desire and frustration, mostly homosexual, and that this was governing who got jobs and who played where and who succeeded or who failed.

It was so different to her own world. She had managed to leave the very dull, very depressing place where they had trained her how to sell cosmetics so well that she firmly believed she could sell lip-gloss to men with beards. She had always wanted to be in business for herself but with no capital it looked impossible. Her father hadn't wanted her to leave the cosmetic people. He thought she should thank her lucky stars day and night for the good luck she had got in life. Her father had never had much luck, there were more weeks when he collected money from welfare than from an employer. Her mother had worked regularly and quietly in a restaurant. She said that her one ambition was that Sophie should never have a job which meant walking and standing, and dealing with dirty plates and difficult customers. She was happy when Sophie was selling nice, fresh, good-smelling oils and paints for people's faces. She was worried when she seemed to become a person of no account sitting in a little stall shouting her wares to the public.

Sophie sighed, thinking how little everyone around her knew about business. If she had been her father, she would have kept a steady job; if she had been her mother, she would have demanded to be a cashier in that restaurant, where she could have sat in a little glass box near the door, rather than get varicose veins by walking and standing; if she were Eddie, she *would* take any acting job anywhere if she wanted to act, or more probably she would decide that if acting didn't want her among its ranks, she would take some other job and act in her spare time. Really she had made very little impression on anyone, with her own business-like attitudes. Nobody realized that it wasn't easy to be organized and disciplined, and to make money. It took a lot of time, and worry, and ate into all those hours you could be sitting around and enjoying yourself. Nobody ever got drawn into her little belief that people might be here on earth to work hard. Nobody but Peggy. Peggy was her one success.

Peggy had been a mess, and Sophie thought she would always be one, but she was so warm and friendly, that you looked through all this bamboo curtain of rubbish and saw a lovely, big, responsive soul inside. Peggy had been to the same school, had done the same useless meaningless course in 'Business administration'. Well, hardly done it, Peggy had barely attended a class there. She had been in chip-shops and coffee-shops, and places with plastic table tops where people ate ice-creams and drank fizzy drinks instead of learning Business administration or delivering bundles of dresses from the wholesale house to the retail which was what they were being paid for.

Peggy had a year of liberty, then came the storm. Her mother couldn't understand why she wasn't fitted for a wonderful job, some high business post. Gradually the tales of the chip-shops emerged, and Peggy left home under the darkest cloud you could find, a cloud of ingratitude.

Sophie had seen her from time to time. Usually she came to borrow a few pounds. More often than not Sophie got them back. Sometimes she came to grumble. This man had let her down, that man hadn't told her he was married, the other man had been perfectly nice for a fortnight and then it turned out that all he wanted was to beat her and for her to beat him. She worked in Woollies for a while and was sacked for stealing. She thought that this was unfair. Sophie thought it was also pretty unfair to steal from Woollies, and Peggy only grudgingly agreed.

She worked for a while in one of the coffee-shops of her youth. Sophie always had coffee there just to have a chat.

Sometimes she thought it mightn't be such a good idea. Peggy looked weary, and dirty, and beaten, she seemed to resent Sophie's smart looks, essential for her trade, and her smart little car essential for bringing her trade from door to door.

But still Peggy didn't have anyone else, and when she was arrested the first time and charged with being drunk and disorderly, Sophie was the one she sent for. She sent for Sophie when she was in hospital, too, suffering, they told her, from malnutrition. Sophie came when she was charged with soliciting, and when she was finally sent to prison on her third charge, it was Sophie who waited for her three weeks later in the little car and drove her back home.

When Peggy immediately retrieved a bottle of barley-wine that she had hidden in the hallway of the depressing house where she lived, Sophie decided she had had enough. Quite enough. There they were sitting in this filthy room, and she was refusing a glass of cloudy, muddy-looking drink with the excuse that it was a bit early in the day. Her old friend Peggy had become a prostitute, a thief, and a near-alcoholic.

The years of dragging herself up and away and onwards were looking useless, if she could be dragged down again so quickly by Peggy. She lost her temper, and said all this and more.

'I'm not just dumping you, because I've become all up-in-the-air,' she shouted eventually. 'Stop telling me that I have ideas above myself. I've no ideas for God's sake, I just work bloody hard, and it isn't easy and everyone around me seems afraid of work or . . . or sneers at it and at me. So now I'm telling you I'm sick of it, sick, sick, sick. I have no more pity for you. I haven't any more words, any more "Poor things" to say to you. You can go whatever bloody way you like, I don't care if I never hear about you again, because every time I hear from you you want something, money, help, someone to take you home from gaol. If you don't want something at the beginning, you end up wanting something. You drain me, and make me feel weak and feel nothing. So to hell with you Peggy, to hell with you, I'm sick of you.'

And then it was Sophie not Peggy who cried. Peggy was amazed. Not upset, just amazed.

The great cool Sophie was sitting there crying, the calm Sophie had shouted. The mask had slipped. Peggy was transfixed. Instead of the list of excuses, explanations, and life's miseries that normally fell out unasked for, she heard herself say quite calmly:

'What would you like me to do?'

'I'd like you to look after yourself for a change and not rely on me to look after you. I'd like you to do something quite extraordinary for you, that's go out and earn a bloody living like most people in the world.'

Sophie gathered up her bag and her car keys and banged out of the dirty room in the depressing house, and went off and sold cream that took lines from under your eyes to women who ran small dress shops. In and out of her car she got, dragging display literature, explaining that people who bought dresses would like to have unlined faces to wear with them. She went on and on until the last late-closing shop had closed, then returned to her flat and worked on reports until midnight and went to sleep.

Next day Peggy was at her door. A tidier Peggy, not drunk, not hungover, not pleading.

'Can I come with you on your rounds?' she asked simply.

Sophie was tired. 'Yes, if you don't talk,' she said, and the day was much like any other, except for the vaguely comforting feeling of Peggy sitting silently beside her. They hardly spoke a word to each other until lunch-time. Then Sophie offered her a drink.

'I'll have a coffee,' said Peggy.

During the coffee Peggy had asked intelligent questions about the kind of stores, shops and boutiques they had been visiting. She wanted to know how much credit they got. Since Peggy couldn't have had a pound note to her name, Sophie wondered at the drift of the conversation. Surely Peggy couldn't see herself as a shop-owner, even if she were going to pull herself together? But anything was better than the kind of thing Peggy normally talked about, so Sophie answered her sensibly. Sophie was also relieved that no malice seemed to be directed towards her for yesterday's outburst.

Peggy came silently in the car with Sophie for about a week, except for the day she had to go and see a probation officer or social worker. She didn't have any tales to tell about these visits, no theories about how women in such jobs were sadists. Sophie began to feel quite optimistic about her, but didn't want to rock any boat by saying it was a useless way to spend your days, sitting in someone else's car. Perhaps Peggy was just desperately lonely, she thought.

Then Peggy came up with her suggestion. She wondered, would these women in the shops buy handmade bags?

Sophie's first thought was that Peggy was planning to steal the bags, but no, she said, she had learned a bit of leather work once, and it turned out she was quite good at it. Would Sophie like to come and see some of it that evening?

The dirty and untidy bedroom was still untidy, but not with clothes, make-up and empty barley-wine bottles. This time it was with bits of leather and cord. Sophie stood transfixed.

Because the bags in all sorts of shapes and sizes were beautiful.

Some of them were soft pinks and blues, others were bold blacks and whites. They were made on a patchwork system, because Peggy had only enough money for scraps, she said. She looked shyly at Sophie, and blushed with pleasure at the evident delight and surprise she saw.

'I was wondering, could I earn a living selling them?' asked Peggy as timidly as a child. Sophie's heart was so full of pride and delight and resolution that she hardly trusted herself to speak. This must be the way teachers feel, or nurses when their patients get better, she thought; and they sat down and made plans for Peggy's new career.

Things moved very quickly after that; the only problem was that Peggy couldn't keep up with the demand. One boutique took a dozen, and rang up three days later for three dozen more. Sophie spent a whole Sunday with Peggy working out what they should do. If she were to get someone else to help her, they would have to halve the money. They had already seen the huge mark-up that shopkeepers put on the bags. It was time to define them as 'luxury items', as 'specialist work'. They got labels made with 'handcrafted by Peggy Anderson' on them, and they charged three times the price. They got it. And Peggy was in business.

So great was the business that Sophie decided she would abandon cosmetics for it, and that is why she was sitting in her little stall near Marble Arch. Not all the bags were Peggy's, no one person could keep up with that demand. But she sold six of Peggy's a week, and she paid Peggy ten pounds a bag, everyone was happy.

Now that Sophie had time off from the endless reports, and shop calls, and fights about commission that had made up her working life, she was able to have a social life. This was something she hadn't seen much of in the hard years of the cosmetic world. But it wasn't hard to find. There was George, silly, dull, kind George who wanted to marry her six weeks after he met her, and who took her to tennis parties and to drink outside Hooray Henry bars, where everyone talked about the last or the next tennis party, and what car everyone else was driving.

And then there was Michael, who was kind and dull too. And Fred who was far from dull, but also very selfish and made no bones about telling her that he would like a wife doing something a little more classy than working as a hawker on Oxford Street. And suddenly one night there was Eddie. At the theatre on a summer evening, when Fred had gone to get the drinks and they had started talking about the play, Eddie had asked if she was an actress, and on impulse she had told him exactly where her little shop was, hoping he would call there. He did, and they drifted into friendship, and an affair that became a real love affair, and then it seemed only right that Eddie should live with her, and now she couldn't live without Eddie.

It was for Eddie that she got up early in the mornings because bills were bigger for two. It was for Eddie that she begged Peggy to make more bags, since the Peggy Andersons were the sure-fire sellers. It was for Eddie that she closed the shop for an hour and went off to the Berwick Street market to buy each night's dinner.

People told her that she had become nicer since she met Eddie. Her tired mother, whose veins were like knots of rope nowadays, and her sad-eyed father, both said she was more cheerful these days, but they put it down to her feckless life among the traders rather than to any love or warmth that had been added. They still thought her foolish to have thrown up her chances of real money.

Peggy said she looked marvellous, better than the days when she used to wear all the make-up she was selling. Love was great, said Peggy gloomily, for those lucky enough to find it. But Peggy didn't seem to like Eddie. She thought he was lazy and that he took too much from Sophie.

'I don't trust him,' she had said once. 'He's one of the takers. I should know, I used to be one. He'll take all you can give, and then one day he'll decide you are nagging, or not enough fun, or not sexy enough, and he'll go and take from someone else.'

Sophie had just laughed. 'Nothing worse than a re-formed drunk for telling you the evils of having a glass of sherry.'

Peggy simply shrugged. 'Don't say I didn't warn you,' she said, and went back to her leather cutting. She worked now about ten hours a day. Whenever Sophie called, she was either bent over minute pieces of leather or she was out. Looking for pieces from her various outlets, she said, or having a walk to clear her head. Sophie was amazed that she could change lifestyles so simply but Peggy said that she mustn't be naive. Occasionally she visited Mr Shipton in the afternoons, he had a couch in his office, and Mr Shipton was very nice about giving Peggy pieces of leather and suede from his factory, so Peggy was very nice to him from time to time on his office couch.

Sophie found that sad and a bit disgusting, but Peggy said rubbish, it was glorious compared to picking people up in the streets, and how else could she afford all the material, so Sophie tried to put it out of her mind.

But today her mind was troubled as she sat and smiled at the tourists and made the odd sale. She felt very restless and anxious for something to change. It wasn't just the heat and the headache, it was as if she had been getting ready for this feeling. Systematically she ticked off all the good things about the way she lived. She had Eddie, beautiful tender Eddie, with his big dark eyes that made her feel weak just thinking about them, like girls were meant to go weak at the knees over pop stars. Eddie was so moody and marvellous that you never knew what to expect when you got home in the evenings. But that's what made the evenings when he had bought her a huge bunch of lilac, and was waiting in his black dressing-gown to take her straight to bed . . . so magic. It quite paid for the other evenings when he wasn't in, and came in sulkily slamming the door, because yet another fairy casting-director had wanted his body, not his acting.

The only time they talked about the future was about Eddie's future. There had been that time he nearly got a part in a show going to the States, and Sophie had become so excited and said she must get Peggy working overtime to make enough bags so that she could sell them there. Eddie had been firm that she mustn't leave her place in Marble Arch, and that it would only be a couple of months' separation. She had loved him for being so solicitous about her work.

At school they used to have a teacher who always made them 'count their blessings'. Sophie remembered that it had been a hard thing to do in those days when she wanted to look like a model, and live in a house with a swimming pool. Nowadays it wasn't really all that much easier. Blessings should be accepted, not counted. So she had Eddie, so she had her health, apart from the odd bad headache. So she had a way of earning a living that she enjoyed. At the age of twenty-seven she was in business for herself, few other women could boast that. Even if Peggy became unreliable again, she still had plenty of other people who made bags. What could be wrong with her?

A couple stopped and picked up one of Peggy's bags. They examined the label and gave funny little cries of recognition.

'That's the girl we met at the theatre yesterday,' said the woman. 'Peggy Anderson, she said she made bags, these are lovely.'

'Do you know Peggy?' asked Sophie with interest. Peggy never mentioned anyone at all except the awful man whom she met on the couch now and then.

'Yes,' said the man, who seemed a nice chatty kind of fellow, but to Sophie's practised eye, a chatty fellow who would be nice to meet and who would buy nothing. 'We went to this lunch-time play yesterday, and got talking to a girl in the wine-bar, she was waiting for her fellow to turn up. Very good-looking girl, lovely red hair.'

'They are awfully dear,' said the woman sadly. 'But they are lovely. Are there any others of hers a bit cheaper?'

'What was the play?' asked Sophie suddenly, knowing somehow that they were going to say *The Table-lighter*, a silly little play which Eddie had seen yesterday. He had said it was a silly little play because he hadn't got a part in it. He had also said he had gone to it with Garry, a friend of his who was an agent, a useless agent. Peggy must have gone with Eddie, she didn't know anyone else, but why had neither of them mentioned it?

'It was *The Table-lighter*,' said the woman. 'This Peggy says she usually goes out at lunch-time, it takes her mind off work, and her chap is an actor, very good-looking fellow. He was late because he had been seeing someone about a job, I think.'

'It's a small world,' said the man.

'It is indeed,' agreed the woman.

'Oh very small,' said Sophie. 'Did they seem very close, Peggy and this actor? I just ask because I used to be rather worried about her, you know, she didn't seem to have much social life . . . I was wondering whether this might be something, well, you know, serious . . .'

Her heart was pounding, and she felt strangely outside herself as she asked the question. How great it was to be so cool and calm and not to panic, when the world was falling down. This is what she must have been expecting all morning.

'I don't think so, do you?' said the woman to her husband. 'Not a real thing going, they just seemed to be great friends laughing and joking without a care in the world. It's incredible to think that he's an actor and she's a leather worker like this. They didn't seem to have a care in the world.'

The nice man put the bag down. £20 was too much even for the work of someone he had met.

'That's right, I felt that too, sort of carefree. But then you know there are people who can be like that, and something sort of looks after them. It's like as if there were a big smiling God who says, "Go on Peggy and Eddie, amuse yourselves, I'll look after you".'

They couldn't know as they looked at the steely green eyes of the little girl in the bag shop that they were looking into the face of a big smiling God, who didn't know how to stop smiling.

Bond Street

The light was very bright when Margaret came out of the station. Everything seemed to dazzle her. Even the daffodils on sale in big baskets seemed too harsh a yellow. People's spring clothes seemed too loud, and the buses must have been re-sprayed recently. Surely they were never so aggressively red before? Or was it because there were so many of them in Oxford Street?

She was a little tired, she often felt tired before she began a shopping spree, it was tension she supposed. Nobody liked shopping, places were too crowded, assistants not at all helpful, so many foreigners who didn't even attempt to speak English properly. Shopping was hardly something you did for fun. But then Margaret did shopping slightly differently from most people. She didn't actually pay for the goods she brought home. Her tensions and frustrations came not from trying to catch the eye of a shop assistant, but from avoiding it.

She made a list, like any conventional shopper would do. She took a shopping bag, she always carried enough money to pay for these listed items, but rarely if ever broke into it. She paused and window-shopped. She had coffee when her feet were tired, she got into little chats with other resting shoppers. In the evening she would go home again, sighing a little on the underground until someone would stand and give her a seat. Margaret had shopped in London like this once a month for nine years. Never in those nine years had she come into contact with a store detective, a security man, or anyone remotely suspicious of her.

Blinking slightly in the sunlight, she looked at her list.

Red towels.

Knives.

Tights.

Remnants.

Pendant.

Giant cup.

Table-lighter.

Jacket.

A lot of them could be 'bought' in Selfridges, but she wanted a jacket from Marks, and she had seen a nice table-lighter in a small souvenir-type shop on her last visit. She might go down to Liberty's for the remnants. She made sure that her wallet with the eighty-four pounds in it was safely zipped into the pocket inside her coat. You couldn't be too careful these days, with teams of pickpockets coming to London from abroad. She straightened her shoulders and went off to buy towels.

She had painted the bathroom last week. Harry had been delighted with it. He said it looked really cheerful with all that white and the window-frame red. He was going to buy a nice cheerful red-and-white bath-mat, he promised.

'And I'll get some red towels, when I'm doing my shopping,' Margaret had said.

'Aren't towels a bit dear?' Harry had wondered with a frown coming over his big kind face.

'Not if you shop around, they would be if you bought the first good ones you saw,' said Margaret.

'I don't know what I'd do without you, you're a great little shopper,' Harry had beamed, and Margaret felt safe when she saw his frown disappear. She felt very frightened when Harry worried, he looked so old.

The towels were easy. You pick up a big one, a middle-size one and two small ones, you take them out under the light to examine them properly, so that you have separated them from the big piles where they are stacked. Then moving slowly, and concentrating on them carefully, looking neither left nor right, you move farther and farther away from their original place. Put down your shopping bag and examine the corners of the towels to see that they are properly finished, drop the smaller ones into the bag on the ground, never looking around, that's the secret, then in a business-like way fold the big one into a small manageable size and put it in on top of the others, walking with the bag held out in front of you towards the desk where it says PAY HERE. Anyone watching you would think you are taking the items to pay for them, people at PAY HERE never watch anything at all. You then ask the PAY HERE people where curtains are, and if, suppose, by some terrible chance you are stopped . . . then you say, 'I went straight to the Pay place, and I got so absorbed in the curtains that I simply forgot.'

Margaret didn't know what would happen if she were caught. She assumed she would be able to talk herself out of it, if there were only one item in her bag, which was why she worked on the time-consuming principle of taking only one thing, and then checking it in as a parcel or in a left-luggage locker. *That's* what made shopping so tiring for her, all the endless walking backwards and forwards to luggage lockers, but it seemed only sensible. The day she was lazy was certainly the day she would be caught.

No problem either with the knives. Nice steak knives with wooden handles, Harry would love these. She would say she had found them in the attic, that they were a present for an anniversary, a present which must have got tidied away. They would laugh together over their good fortune in having found them.

The tights were a luxury for herself. She still had good legs and she hated the kind of stockings that looked cheap and hairy. Every month she collected four or five pairs of nice sheer tights, sometimes in what they called 'the new fashion shades'. She never mentioned these to Harry. He would occasionally say, 'You've got better legs than half these women on the television,' and she would smile happily.

The remnants were for dressmaking. She wasn't very good at it, but anyone could sew a pillow-case or a cushion cover, and it made Harry feel happy and comfortable, looking over at his wife sewing away contentedly while they watched television. She took enough to make a tablecloth too. That would only need a hem around it and Harry would never look at the edges, just at the nice bright colour on the table at breakfast, and he might say, 'Imagine you made that cloth yourself. I don't know how other fellows manage with their wives, I really don't.'

The pendant was a present for their son Jerry, who was away in the North at university. It would be his birthday next week. Jerry was a worry to her, he often looked at her very hard without saying anything.

'What are you thinking about?' she'd ask.

'Nothing, Mum,' came the invariable reply, but she felt that he was staring at her, and pitying her somehow and worrying about her. She didn't like that at all.

Once she had sent him a cashmere sweater for his birthday and he had rung up not so much to thank her as to protest.

'They cost a fortune, Mum, however did you afford it? They cost half what Dad earns in a week.'

Margaret realized she had gone too far.

'I bought it in an Oxfam shop,' she said, pretending to confess to a little economy, but her heart was pounding with fear.

'But it's new, it's all wrapped up in cellophane,' argued Jerry.

'Someone gave it away, a present they didn't want.'

'They must have been mad,' grumbled Jerry, still suspicious. From then on, it had to be gifts that nobody could put a real price on. The pendant would have cost about £7 had she paid for it, but she hadn't of course because she had asked the nice young man to show her some earrings and put the pendant in her pocket as he went to get an earring tray.

She and Harry had seen a television play the other night where the husband had his tea out of a huge china cup. Harry had smiled and said wasn't it lovely.

'I've seen those in the shops,' said Margaret. 'Would you like one?'

'No, it's only silly, they cost a fortune and maybe my tea would get cold in it. It just looked nice, that's all.'

Margaret said she had a half-memory of seeing them in a sale where they cost about fifty pence.

'Oh well then,' Harry had said and went back to looking at the television.

The one Margaret took would have cost her seven

pounds fifty pence, but when she was showing it to Harry tonight she would leave out the seven pounds. She thought it was a great deal of money to pay for one cup and saucer. Sometimes she felt aggrieved if the items she took were very expensive. She liked the best, but she liked things to be good value.

The table-lighter was a present for Harry's brother and his wife, who were having a twenty-fifth anniversary party next week. Harry's brother Martin never approved of Margaret, something Harry wouldn't and couldn't see in a million years. The families met rarely. A cursory visit around Christmas time, another in the summer. Martin's wife never had a cigarette out of her mouth, she never wore stockings, her hair was a mess, she had a loud laugh. Margaret was glad not to see too much of her. But she was always charming when they came to the house, and laughed insincere little peals when Martin said to his brother, 'Well, she has you rightly tamed, Harry, never thought I'd see the day when you'd be out planting vegetables and filling window-boxes.'

'Harry's marvellous at gardening, he grows a great deal of what we eat,' Margaret would say loyally.

'That's how you must be able to afford this place,' Martin had once said, looking around at lamps, ornaments, vases, and linen tray-cloths, all carried home from Margaret's monthly shopping trips.

'I don't know how you afford this style, I really don't.'

Martin had been far from helpful over that bad business years ago. Far from standing up for her and trying to keep up a good name for them, he had encouraged Harry in all that silliness.

'Never thought you had it in you,' he laughed coarsely, when Margaret had called a family conference to deal with the situation. 'A young lassie too, well that beats everything.' Martin's sluttish wife had let the cigarette ash fall down her stained cardigan with excitement. Old Harry, and a young girl from the factory, and a baby on the way. Excitements like that didn't come very often.

Margaret wondered whether the table-lighter was too good for them. After all they would have humiliated her, set her adrift if they had their way. Why should she get them anything? But still, it was all part of the scheme, the plan, the whole elaborate complicated business that made her victory assured. She had to be the perfect sister-in-law as well as the perfect wife. Only a perfect sister-in-law, herself a non-smoker, would be so thoughtful as to give something like a table-lighter. So quietly it went into the bag. Later she would get a really cheap box for it, they would assume it had cost a couple of quid instead of twenty. They would be surprised it worked so well. Part of Margaret's good taste.

It would be a dull evening at their anniversary. Their children were loud too, and drank beer from cans. The lazy wife would make a small attempt at food, but it might only be sandwiches and trifle. There would be a lot of drink of course. And sometime in the evening Martin would nudge Harry and ask him were there any more little girls that he could pass on to his old brother, and Harry would look sheepish and silly and hope that Margaret hadn't heard.

Martin would love Margaret to have her come-uppance even at this late stage. He couldn't believe how well she had managed that business years ago. Looking back on it, Margaret herself often wondered how she had been able to cope with it.

There was Harry, all shuffling and foolish, and not able to look at anyone. There was this girl, small, fat, very fat now that she was five months pregnant. There was her father, a bit older than Harry, and even more shuffling, and everyone shouting about money, and rights and duties, and doing the proper thing, and not letting anyone get away with anything. Until Margaret had spoken.

'The only decision we have to make is this,' she had said. 'If Harry accepts that he is the father of this child, then he must marry the lady as soon as possible and give the child a name and a home. I will take our son and this house, and whatever it costs for both of us to live here. Harry must provide for two families, he will have no access to my home. I'm sure with overtime, he'll earn enough to keep us all.'

Her voice sounded so calm that everyone stopped shouting, and listened. Martin and his wife had been invited especially to give more support, but they sat open-mouthed through it all.

'If Harry thinks that he is only one of several people who might be the baby's father, then he should give the lady some money towards the upkeep of the child – a small lump sum, to thank her for his pleasure, and to acknowledge some limited degree of responsibility.'

The room was silent.

'And what about you Margaret?' asked Harry. 'What will you do?'

'If you leave our home, and go with this lady to some room, I will never see you, nor allow you to see Jerry as long as I live. If you fail in your payments, I will get a court order against you. I have to look after *my* child, just as this lady has to look after hers. If you decide that you cannot be the sole person to be named as father, and you pay this lady a sum of money, to be agreed between you and her and her father, then when everybody has gone, I will make your supper as usual, and I will live here with you, never mentioning this whole incident again, unless you want to.'

'You'd forgive me?' stumbled Harry.

'It's not a question of forgiving, there's nothing to forgive, it's the bargain we made when we got married. I give you a comfortable home, and you give me your presence and loyalty, and support me. There's nothing unusual about it at all.'

And she had gone out into the kitchen to put some flowers in water, while their voices came from the sitting-room, and then they all left. Nobody came in to say good-bye or to tell her what had happened.

There had been no sound from the sitting-room, and she didn't know whether Harry had left with them. The five minutes were like five hours, the clock ticked, and the water tank burbled, loudly, menacingly. But she wouldn't run in to see was he there, had he stayed, had she won.

She tore the stems of the flowers to little green rags as she waited. She knew this was some kind of test. It was too long, he must have gone. If she had lost, what would she do with the house. There was no point in scraping and saving to make it nice, just for a ten-year-old boy, and herself. If she had won, she would really keep her promise, she would make it a wonderful home for him, for them. Even if she had to steal, she thought, she wouldn't back-track on her word.

Then the door of the kitchen opened, and Harry, red-eyed, came in.

'I'm giving her £50,' he said.

'That seems very fair,' said Margaret.

She never asked why, or whether he had loved the girl, or whether she was a marvellous lay, or how and when they had met. She kept her bargain, and the next time she had gone to Oxford Street, she started bringing home little treats for Harry and herself. Her reward was his guilty devoted smile, his belief that he had married a Wonder-woman and nearly lost her through his own stupidity. That made her feel very good.

There was only the jacket left now; everything else, including her coat, was in the left-luggage office. She had a scarf and a brooch in her handbag. That was how she had got the jacket four years ago, the nice lilac one, that Harry had said made her look so young. This time she wanted black velvet.

She took one from the rail, and with one movement removed the price tag, throwing it behind the radiator, and pinned her own brooch on the lapel. The jacket was on her in a flash, with her scarf knotted under its collar. In seconds she had taken a different jacket out to hold it up to the light.

'It's nice,' she said to the sales girl.

'Nice cheerful red,' said the girl.

'And they wear very well,' said Margaret. 'I've had this one for quite a while, I was wondering should I get it in another colour.'

'It's a good idea to buy a couple if they suit you,' said the girl.

'But,' said Margaret, 'I think it's a bit extravagant of me really. I'll just go and do the rest of the shopping and if I've anything left over I'll come back later.'

'That's a good idea,' said the girl politely.

And she walked out into the afternoon sunlight to collect all the shopping from the left-luggage, and go home to Harry.

Oxford Circus

My heart sank when Frankie got a job in the B.B.C. Up to now all the disasters in her life had been reasonably contained among her ever-dwindling circle of friends. But if she were in reach of a microphone she might easily broadcast them to the nation. They might even become national incidents. Because Frankie was rarely out of trouble. I think it was only because I was such a boss, that I was a friend of hers at all. I liked the self-importance of rescuing her. I liked her undying gratitude and useless promises to be more careful the next time.

Clive didn't like Frankie, which was unusual because Clive liked almost everyone. He said she was brainless. Yet she had a far better degree than any of us. He said she liked getting into trouble, but he hadn't seen the tears pouring down her face as she sat in the police-station wrongly accused of starting a fight in a restaurant and causing a breach of the peace. Frankie hadn't started the fight, she had tried to stop somebody else's. Clive said she was vain. That couldn't be right either. Would somebody who was vain turn up at a dinner party in filthy painting clothes, because she had become so involved in doing up a neighbour's child's playroom that she had forgotten to look at her watch and just ran out to catch a taxi the way she was?

Frankie had recently disentangled herself from a particularly horrible man, who owned a restaurant and a bad temper, and who had beaten Frankie very badly on three separate occasions. The day she said she was leaving him, he had taken some of her best clothes and burned them in his incinerator.

She had taken nothing from the horrible man except a few bruises and a series of misunderstood memories. That was another fault of Frankie's, she never learned from anything. If she were to fall down and pass out six nights in succession because she had drunk too much, she never considered for one moment that there was an element of cause and effect. She just regarded each falling-down as a terrible happening to be deeply regretted. There would be other restaurant-owners who would throw all her clothes into the incinerator. I just hoped there wouldn't be many of them in the B.B.C

'I want a reduction in the licence fee,' was all Clive said when I told him that Frankie was going to work at Broadcasting House. 'The thought of that woman's voice coming at me from the radio is enough to make me take sick-leave.'

Clive can be very silly once he has a bee in his bonnet about something, so I took no notice except to say that she would be doing research, not actually speaking on the air.

'That's a mercy,' said Clive. 'But the number of apologies for whatever she has researched for some unfortunates will be legion.'

For once we were having a quiet night at home, and I had cooked a dinner. Usually neither of us have much time, what with Clive giving evening classes and me taking them. For once we decided not to study but to stick photos into an album, and we had them all out on the floor when the doorbell rang. In London that's unusual. We hadn't invited anyone, and nobody selling bibles or double-glazing would ever climb the stairs to our flat, however great the commission in this world or the next.

It was Frankie.

'I'm not going to stay a minute, I'll leave the door open so that I won't even be tempted,' she said, blocking the door open with her handbag and creating such a draught that all the photos blew out of their little piles.

'Close the bloody door,' said Clive and I knew the evening was ruined.

'I just wanted to borrow one sweater, and one skirt. Until lunchtime tomorrow only. To go to work in, the job starts tomorrow you see, and because Bernard burned all my things I've got nothing to wear except this dress, which I don't think would be suitable for the Beeb.'

It was a lovely dress, cut to the navel, with rhinestones all around the bit of bosom it had. It would be unusual in the B.B.C. but might just hasten on the disaster that was bound to befall Frankie. I said cheerfully that I would go and see what I could find.

Frankie sat on the floor, falling out of her rhinestones and oohing and aahing at the pictures.

'My God, didn't we all look foul at your wedding?' she shouted, and even through the bedroom door I could feel Clive bristling.

Then.

'Clive, that's not you. I don't believe it. With all the curls and the little toy horse sitting on a stool. It's beautiful.' She positively gurgled over the picture. I had begged him once with tears in my eyes not to throw it out, and had won only by such a small margin that I had always kept it hidden in the bottom of the drawer. I took it out to gurgle a bit myself over, privately.

I rushed out of the bedroom carrying my only good skirt and a new blouse which I had not yet worn.

'Would these do?' I said hurriedly.

Frankie was so far into the photos now that nothing would have got her out of them.

'Look at that picture of you and me and Gerry!' she exclaimed happily. 'Do you remember that night you went out with him and I had to pretend to your mother that you stayed with me? It was awful, I kept getting so confused about what I was meant to have been doing, or what we were meant to have been doing, that I'm sure I gave the game away.'

Oh she had, she had, then and now, but that was Frankie, so innocent, and hopeless. Always.

'I believe you have joined the B.B.C.,' said Clive in a heavy overdone effort to save me embarrassment. It was as if he had flashed a notice saying let us change this unsavoury subject of my wife's past. I hated him for it.

Even Frankie must have sensed some tension, because

she sort of gathered up her limbs, and breathed a few dizzy remarks about hoping she'd cope with her first day as a new girl, and snatched my clothes and ran.

Clive had put away the photos. The one of him with curls he had torn into eight pieces, and thrown into the basket. He said he had remembered he had a lot of study to catch up on. I went to bed in a sulk, couldn't sleep, so got up and did the ironing. Clive said I was behaving like a martyr, that I was only ironing to make him feel guilty. No, I said, harassed working wives love ironing, it keeps them sane, they use it as therapy in mental hospitals, everyone knows that. He said I was becoming as childish as my friend Frankie, and even more immature. I said his shirts were now a size too small for him, or a half size anyway, why else would all the top buttons be loose?

Oh it was a lovely evening.

Frankie rang me at work, nobody except Frankie ever rings me at work. The Principal hates it, and he's right, you can hear the whole form screaming while you're out of the classroom. I've told Frankie this again and again, but she never remembers. She wanted to meet me at six o'clock to give me back my clothes.

'I don't need them at once,' I said, furious to have brought the Principal's wrath down on me again for nothing.

'But I want you to have a little drink, just two little drinks in the B.B.C. Club,' she said beseechingly.

There was no time to chat. I could hear a noise like a tank division coming from my classroom. Anyway I'd always wanted to go into the B.B.C. Club, that's what did it.

'Yes,' I shouted. 'Where is it?'

'Get off at Oxford Circus, and walk in a straight line,' she said. 'I'll have your clothes in a nice plastic bag ready for you.'

I hoped that she'd remember to get some replacements for herself. I could only too easily see her sitting there in her bra and pants drinking a pink gin.

The real reason I gave in so easily was that I wanted to avoid meeting Clive. We had parted in a mutual sulk that morning and I didn't look forward to apologizing or waiting for him to. It would do him good not to see me waiting there anyway. We usually had a beer and a sandwich from the fridge at about six, before he went out to teach a lot of foolish self-advancing housewives all about economics, and before I went to learn Italian. I was doing a degree in Italian so that I could teach it in a school where the children were older, and more appreciative, and didn't scream like deprived railway engines.

Two little drinks at six o'clock, and the chance of seeing some personalities . . . it was a great idea.

The B.B.C. Club was huge, and had two separate entrances, each with a porter's desk where you had to show an identity card before being let in.

'Perhaps your friend has signed you in,' said a porter kindly, examining the visitors' book. My friend hadn't There was no passport to personalities for me at all. I felt very sad.

I waited on a chair, feeling foolish, for about half an hour until Frankie arrived, breathless. She was desperately sorry but she'd been to the shops, it was late closing, and she'd got herself something to wear instead of my skirt and blouse.

She had indeed. It was an outfit of skin-tight black velvet pants and a sort of a big red handkerchief tied under her bosom. It looked great, but it didn't look like the kind of thing she could wear the next day at work. I had grave doubts whether it was even the kind of thing she should wear in this club.

We were about to sweep in when the porter asked for her card.

'But I work in the B.B.C.,' said Frankie proudly.

'I'm afraid you have to be a member of the club though,' he said kindly.

Frankie was like a toddler whose ice-cream had been snatched away. I thought she was going to cry.

'We can go to a pub,' I said.

'I don't want to go to a pub, I want to go in here, it's where all the B.B.C. people go,' said Frankie in a five-year-old voice.

At that moment a couple of men were waiting for the porter to finish so that they could go in, and they were amused by Frankie's predicament. They asked her what programme she worked on, and good-naturedly signed us both in, looking at Frankie's outfit appreciatively.

We were in. It was a big room, hot and smoke-filled, and crowded with people. I couldn't see anyone I had ever seen on television, and I wasn't near enough to people to hear any famous voices from radio either. I was a bit disappointed.

Frankie had wriggled up to the bar and got us drinks. There was nowhere to sit, nowhere to lean even, so we stood in the middle of a crowded room, like people at a party where we knew no one. I didn't like it at all.

'I have a purpose in coming here,' hissed Frankie, looking left and right in case anyone was listening.

'Oh my God,' I said.

'No, listen, you're always getting frightened over nothing. I think you don't go out enough, you and Clive. I mean poring over old baby pictures every night, it's not natural.'

'We won't be doing that again for a while,' I said darkly.

Frankie didn't notice any nuance in my tone. She was far more interested in her purpose.

'I'm here for a special reason,' she said again. Anyone who knew Frankie even slightly could see that trouble lay ahead. I who had known her since school felt weighed down with doom.

'You see there's this guy, my boss on the programme. He's absolutely great, very dynamic, people just do anything he says, and he was saying today that he thought I was getting on very well for someone who had just come in. I really did, you know. I used my initiative and brought many more files than they asked for, and we found a whole new line to go on . . .'

'Go on about the guy,' I said resignedly.

'Well, he said that what I needed was someone to sort of talk me into the programme, let me know the feel of the place, what they were at, where they were going, and what they wanted to do. And he said that I should try to live and breathe the programme constantly, thinking up new ideas, new ways of dealing with them, that's what makes a programme great he says. Martin says.'

'So?' I said.

'So I thought I should start doing it straight away,' beamed Frankie.

'Are we going to look for people from the programme and start living it and breathing it?' I asked in disbelief.

'No ... not exactly. You see the one to tell me is this boss man, Martin. He really IS the programme. I thought I'd meet him here and get to know him, off-duty.'

'But if you're going to meet him, why am I here?' I said, hurt.

The two little drinks didn't seem such a good idea now I thought Frankie was going to dash off and leave me at any moment with over half an hour to kill before going to my Italian class.

But that wasn't it, there was more.

'No, he's much too important for me just to turn up here and strike up a chat with him about the programme. That would be very forward. It's more complicated than that.'

I sighed.

'Some of the others were telling me that he has this utter dragon of a wife, a real Tartar woman, who won't let him out of her sight. She works in the Beeb, too, but in another department and she won't let him have any fun. She comes in here every night and stares across the room at him with awful eyes; then at seven o'clock she marches him home for dinner like a school boy.'

I automatically looked at the clock as if to count the minutes before this ritual took place.

'You've only got a half an hour,' I said jokingly.

Frankie was utterly serious.

'I know, that's why I have to find her. I must strike up a friendship with her as soon as possible, so that she'll realize she has nothing to worry about, that I'm not after her husband. If she and I became friends then it would all be fine.'

I looked at Frankie, in her flame-coloured top and her tight, tight pants, her hair falling over her face like someone who had just got out of bed and was waiting, slightly tousled, for the next lover. I didn't think her mission was going to be possible. But there's no use explaining some things to Frankie so I offered to get another drink, and plunged into a sea of bodies around the bar.

When I came back Frankie was gone, or I thought she

was, but she had only gone out to make a phone-call.

'I have to identify her first,' she said. At that moment someone was paged over the loudspeaker.

'That's her,' giggled Frankie.

'Where?' I scanned the room.

'We'll see. I went out to a public phone-box and rang here asking to speak to her. We'll just have to see who goes out.'

Like schoolchildren, we watched the door. Eventually a small blonde disappeared through it.

'That couldn't be his wife, not monsterish enough,' said Frankie firmly.

'Did they tell you he hasn't slept with her for years, but he can't leave her because of the children or her health?' I asked sourly. I was feeling very annoyed with this childishness, and hated being part of it. I also wondered whether Clive was worried about me. Maybe I should have rung him.

The small blonde came back, shrugging her shoulders at her friends. 'Nobody there apparently,' she said. 'The phone was dead.'

'It is her,' said Frankie in amazement.

'Now Frankie,' I begged. 'Don't go up to that woman and start one of your explanations, you know how people misunderstand your way of talking. It's always happening if you think about it. Why do you have to do it today? Let it go for a day or two. Please, Frankie?'

It was, of course, useless. I hadn't even finished speaking when Frankie had bounded over to the blonde's side.

I was too embarrassed to do anything except stare into my drink, and wish I were a million miles away, or about three miles away, at home with Clive, the row over, forgiven, forgotten, the two of us sitting there listening to records, laughing over it all, and making great plans about how we would see the world eventually. It all seemed so safe, and so much what I wanted compared to standing in this awful place with terrible things going on a few feet away.

I hardly dared look over for fear of what was happening. The small blonde woman was hauntingly familiar. Was she on a telly programme? Was she a film star? How did I know her face so well? Frankie had said something about her being a producer, you don't see producers' faces.

I knew it, I knew it, I was summoned over and introduced. Everyone seemed to be quite happy and relaxed, they always do with Frankie . . . initially.

'Is it your first day in the B.B.C. too?' asked the blonde kindly.

'No, I'm not here, I mean I'm only here because Frankie asked me to have a drink with her after work. I'm just going off to my Italian lesson,' I said, wondering why did I always sound like someone who had never learned English but was trying to pick it up as I went along.

'I'm a teacher actually, in a dreary old school, nothing bright and glittery like his,' I said, wondering why I said it. I preferred the school a million times with its familiarity and chalk and noise to this strange place where you might be standing next to a news-reader and anything could happen.

The blonde seemed nice. Frankie had obviously told her some cock-and-bull story about being lonely and nervous in her job and wanting to get to know colleagues in the Corporation. This had endeared her to all of them. They said that it was only too rare that people admitted to knowing nobody, most people went around and knew nobody for ages because of this English trait of reticence.

One of the men bought us a drink, we were part of a group.

Frankie was making a great effort to convince the blonde that she was a serious, steady person interested only in her job.

'I'm not at all like my teacher friend, always flitting around,' she said. I didn't think anyone could have believed her. There was I in a jumper and skirt, while Frankie looked as if she was about to do a gypsy dance, and strip in the middle of it. They couldn't have believed her, could they? But it was important for Frankie's purpose that they did, so I went along with it.

'Yes, Frankie is always trying to get me to settle down. I couldn't give two pins for my work, just the holidays and the hours are all I could care about. Frankie likes to live and breathe her job, she puts in endless hours of overtime, silly I call it.'

Frankie smiled, the blonde frowned at me.

'You shouldn't stay in teaching, if you don't like it, it's

bad for you and the children. I really do think it's a vocation, half my family are teachers, and the other half used to be. Those of us that didn't do it well got out,' she said.

Inside I agreed with her, but I had to go on, no use in being converted too easily. I'd never see this woman again, and she wouldn't judge Frankie by her hopeless, feckless friend, surely. I'd better make myself a really bad case, whom Frankie was trying to reform.

'Oh I don't know, it's a job the same as any other. Worse paid than a lot, but then you can always read the paper when the kids are doing a test, and our Head is a bit soft about things like doctors' certs. If I want to earn a few quid, real money I mean, in some other job, I just don't turn up for a few days. I get paid just the same.'

Never in my life had I done anything of the sort. One teacher had once, and we were all appalled and shocked. The Principal was a kind man who thought I was a bit flighty sometimes, but only because I did play with the children so much, even after school. His only real grievance was that my classes were too exuberant.

'I'm always trying to make her grow up, to tell her the joys of living and breathing her work,' said Frankie in a goody-goody voice.

'Is it seven?' said the blonde. 'Damn it, I was having a lot of fun. Martin will be around in front of the building in his car, I must run.' She gave Frankie a warm good-bye, and wished her well, hoped to see her again. Barely glancing at me, she said she hoped I'd find a happier job soon.

'I'm really sorry to run,' she said to the others. 'It's just that we have to be home to change, we're going out tonight. My brother's having a little dinner.'

It was only as I saw her side-face on, that I realized why she was so familiar. She was like a twin of my Principal. My nice kind idealistic headmaster, who had, now that I remembered it, a sister who used to be a teacher but who was now a senior producer in the B.B.C.

Tottenham Court Road

A lot of the books seemed to be about lesbians, which wasn't what she wanted, however uninhibited and daring they might be according to the jacket descriptions, and then there were a sizeable number for gay men, with pictures of very beautiful muscled men on the covers, but this again wouldn't be any help. In horrified fascination she saw the section where Alsatian dogs and horses seemed to be people's partners, and about five shelves where people weren't naked at all but clad from head to toe in black leather and brandishing whips.

What she wanted and couldn't find was a book that would tell her how to be an enormous success as a woman in bed with a man. They didn't have any books for twenty-nine-year-old virgins. Such things weren't meant to exist . . . the were an embarrassment to society.

Oh the world was full of books telling twelve-year-olds not to be afraid of menstruation, and telling eight-year-olds about little eggs growing inside mummy's tummy, and assuring seventeen-year-olds that they would go neither blind nor mad from masturbation but that it wasn't as good as a healthy, meaningful, one-to-one sexual relationship. Julia was worn out reading helpful letters to people who complained of being frigid, advising them to relax and to be loving and to specify what they wanted. Who would tell her what she should want, and how to do it at her age without making an utter fool of herself? Twelve, even ten years ago, she could have put herself at the mercy of her seducer, virginity would have been an honour then, something to be treated with respect and awe and tenderness. Nowadays she couldn't possibly tell any would-be seducer that this had never happened before. If it weren't so sad, it would be laughable.

There were no men in raincoats in the shop, no sinister figures with moustaches and sun-glasses salivating over pictures in filthy books. In fact Julia found it very hard to find a book to salivate over herself. They all seemed to be wrapped in cellophane. She wondered how you knew what to buy. There was no way she was going to ask for assistance either from that man who looked as if he should have been a head-gardener in a stately home or from the tired, ageing woman at the cash-desk. She would have to hope that the blurbs, and the overwritten sentences about the material being uncensored, and straight from Scandinavia, would put her on the right trail.

The worst bit was over really, the walking into the shop and settling down with the browsers. She wore a headscarf, which she normally didn't do, in some mad wish to look different, to put on a different personality for this reckless, sinful venture. She had given herself two hours to look for the right book, or maybe books. She had five pounds in her handbag. If it worked it would be an investment well made, and perhaps there was an additional gain, in courage. She would never have believed herself capable of setting off deliberately and examining the outside of pornographic bookshops. She had finally settled on the one which looked as if it had the biggest selection. Really, you could get used to anything, Julia decided. She had now stopped worrying about what the other people in the shop thought about her, and was no longer afraid that they were all going to jump on her and rape her because she had shown herself mad for it by going into a sex shop anyway.

She moved unhappily from the Oral Love section to a small specialist area called Domination. Mainly women in thigh-high boots with evil smiles, and men cowering behind sofas. Disconsolately she leafed through one of the magazines which was open – they had to leave something for you to browse through in those kind of shops – and saw sadly that it was Party Games, and that you would need

111

colouring pencils to work out whose limb belonged to whom.

It was very depressing not to be able to find what she wanted when she had got herself as far as this. Julia had thought that the hard part would be making the decision to find the shop, and going in, and perhaps even understanding the terminology of the book without anyone to practise with, like you could with Yoga or wrestling. She didn't know that her specific requirement would be un-catered for. And it wasn't as if it was easy to know where to go either. She had thought that Soho was the right area to hunt, but fortunately she had been able to ask people at work in a jokey way where they bought sexy magazines, and a knowing guy had said anywhere on Charing Cross Road, in the small places. Much better than Soho, because not priced for tourists. 'Get out at Tottenham Court Road tube station, and you'll be fine then, Julia,' he had said, and the others in the travel-agency had laughed. Because you just didn't associate Julia with poking around in a porn shop. She looked too clean and wholesome and well brought-up.

But they probably assumed that she had at least some kind of sex life, Julia thought in a troubled way. She didn't talk about having one, true, but then neither did anyone else. They were fairly sophisticated there, or even distant about things like that. Katy was married, and Daphne was divorced, and Lorna wasn't married but seemed to have a regular chap called Clive who was mentioned casually in dispatches. They probably thought that Julia met people at week-ends, and maybe went to bed with them. If they knew she didn't, and hadn't, they would have been mildly embarrassed and sorry for her rather than shocked. It was that kind of office.

But her two friends Milly and Paula would have been shocked, and horrified. They were heavily into going to bed with people. Milly regularly with the same, very unavail-able man, whom she said she didn't love, but was irresist-ibly drawn to, and Paula with somebody new and hopeful-sounding every couple of weeks. Julia invented the odd holiday sexual happening, and would feel very trapped when Paula would ask, 'But was he good? I mean, you know, did he *satisfy* you?' Julia would say that some had and some hadn't and this kept Paula happy, and reflective about the differing abilities of men in this field.

Everyone plays games, even with friends, and Julia felt that she would have been breaking all the rules of the game if she had suddenly confessed that she had not known the experience and would they please tell her what it was like from start to finish. Paula and Milly would assume that she was having an early menopause, an unexpected nervous breakdown or had developed unhealthy voyeuristic tendencies that she wanted to indulge. They would never actually believe that such a thing could be true.

And really it was only too easy. Julia had been adamant about not going to bed with Joe, her first and long-lasting boyfriend. She was full of the kind of thought that said in letters of fire that you lost them if you gave into them. She had this firm belief that if she and Joe made love outside marriage he would never trust her again, and that he would assume she would be lifting her skirts for all and sundry. She didn't know from where she got this expression 'lifting her skirts', it was coarse and unlikely and had nothing to do with love. She must have heard her aunt use it about some serving-girl. Her aunt was like that.

Joe had gone to university and found a nice girl there. When he told Julia that their unofficial engagement had now better be forgotten, Julia had asked in a pained way, 'Does she ... er ... sleep with you?' and Joe had laughed lightly and said that there wasn't much chance of actually sleeping with someone at university but they did make love of course.

So Julia, who was now twenty, decided that there must be other standards than her own, but for the next five years the only people who offered her the initiation rights were drunken people, or people who had been stood up or let down by some other girl, and who were using her as a substitute. And suddenly the years were passing, and she never knew what it was like to have the earth move, or to hear wild cries of ecstasy mingling with her own, and she felt frowningly that this was bad news ... Still, there had been so much else to think about, borrowing the money, setting up a different kind of travel agency to anyone else's in a different kind of partnership, going abroad three times a year to investigate things like they all did,

113

and there was getting a flat and doing it up, and keeping her aunt and her father happy by visiting them regularly with lots of cheery stories and bright dismissals of all their ills and complaints. And there was going to the theatre, and meeting Paula and Milly in each other's flats for great meals with lots of wine, and really it was hard to know how the years went by without going to bed with people.

But now it was important. Julia had met a very nice man indeed. He was in publishing and she had met him one evening last year when she was touring the night-clubs of a foreign resort with a notebook, writing down details of atmosphere for next season's brochure. Michael had been sitting in one of the clubs and had seen what she was doing. He offered her a bit of advice about excluding it, because the drinks were too dear and the floor-show was too touristy. Together they roamed several other clubs and at the end of a long night he suggested she come back to his room for a drink. Julia was about to agree when she suddenly realized with a horrible shock that she literally didn't know how to do it. There she was, twenty-eight years old, and she didn't know whether she was meant to lie down on the bed naked and wait for him to do everything, or if she should undress him, or if she should move up and down when it was happening or round and round, and it was all very well to say that she'd learn in time, but who could learn in two minutes what they should have been learning over the last ten years?

Lightly she said no, and refused for the rest of the week also, on the grounds that she didn't go in for holiday things. This sounded, she hoped, as if she went in for real-life things very seriously, and Michael seemed to think that this was reasonable enough. He didn't live in London, but he came to see her for half a dozen week-ends, and for three of those she pretended she had someone staying in the flat and couldn't ask him to stay. Then twice she said she had too much work to do, and didn't want to ask him back. Finally, the last time, she had asked him to the flat for a meal, and when she was getting the usual excuses ready he had held her hand very gently.

'We get on well together,' he had said.

'Sure, very well,' she admitted, almost grudgingly.

'Then why do you close me out?' he asked. He had been

so gentle and understanding that if she had said at that very moment what was worrying her she knew it would have been all right. Why couldn't she? Because she felt foolish. She felt that she was grown-up and intelligent in every way except this. She couldn't bear the vulnerability, it would show. She was even afraid that the whole thing might be messy and might hurt her. Because she was such an ancient virgin, it might be impossible to pierce her virginity. Think how appalling that would be.

She had bought time.

'The next time you come to London you can stay here for the whole week-end,' she said. 'I'd like that. It's just that, well, I'm not ready for it now, and I don't think people who are grown-up and equal should have to make excuses to each other, do you?'

He had agreed, and they had talked of other things, and he had his hand on her neck as they talked, and occasionally he kissed her and told her she was very dear to him. And deep down she thought that it would be possible to lose her virginity before he came back in a few weeks, and it would all be fine from then on.

It's harder than you think to find somebody to sleep with you, in a limited time, and for a limited time and with no strings, and with no build-up. Julia went to a party and behaved outrageously with a businessman who was in London for a few days, having what he said was a whale of a time. She even managed to get him home to her flat. Staring at herself in the bathroom mirror, she wondered whether it could ever have been so terrible for anyone as it was going to be for her. He was very silly and he kept laughing at his own jokes, and he was rather drunk. His idea of romance was to plunge his hand unexpectedly and painfully down the front of her dress. But Julia thought, brushing her gritted teeth in order to be nice and inoffensive for the beautiful act, it was better to learn on someone awful.

When she went back to the sitting-room, he was asleep on the sofa, and no amount of cooing or even shouting could revive him. Eventually she took off his shoes, threw a rug over him, and went to bed in a rage. Next morning she had to make him breakfast, assure him that his wife wouldn't be hurt in any way, and kind of hint that it had all been rather wonderful. She went to the office in a rage also.

In the next ten days she got two more men back to her flat. One was a friend of Lorna's and Clive's who told her eighteen times about his wife having upped and left with a teenager. She promised him consolation and a shoulder, even a whole body, to cry on. First though, there was the story of the wife, over and over, what he had done wrong, what he hadn't done wrong, how he couldn't blame her, how he'd like to throttle her, how he hoped she'd be happy, how he hoped she'd rot in hell. When it was bed-time and Julia got herself into and out of the state of self-pity and self-disgust about making love to such an unlovable man, he said that he would like to lie beside her all night, but that they couldn't make love as he hadn't been able to do that for a long time now. It was quite normal. Apparently the doctor had told him that thousands of men had the same problem.

The other possible bed-mate had been a really loud vulgar friend of Paula's who showed a marginal interest in Julia one night in a pub. Immediately she returned his interest a hundredfold. Since he had been making passes at her unsuccessfully for a couple of years, he was delighted. On the way home he told her what a splendid stud he was, that he wished one could get references for that sort of thing, that he loved women, big women, little women, young women, all women. Julia was nearly in a state of collapse by the time the taxi turned into her street.

'Do you like virgins?' she inquired hopefully.

He did, he loved them, he was very good with them. He hadn't had one for ages now, but he did like virgins.

It was half-way through the drink before deflowering that Julia remembered an article she had read the previous Sunday about venereal disease. It would be just her luck to wait twenty-nine years and then do it for the first time with someone who was riddled with syphilis, and then pass it on the next week to the only man she had ever really wanted. Suddenly she went all funny and said that she couldn't go to bed with him because she thought she had sprained her back. The remark sounded even more stupid than she could have believed possible.

'Let me do all the work,' he had said.

Julia had no idea what he was talking about, but was sure she would catch some disease if she allowed herself to find out. She shooed him out into the night, and decided it would have to be a bookshop.

She had told the girls in the travel agency that she was going to the Family Planning Association, so she would take a long lunch-hour. She had in fact been on the Pill for a month so that she was now protected. All she needed was someone, anyone, who would tell her how not to make an utter fool of herself and drive Michael away next Friday night. It was Tuesday now, for God's sake, she really didn't have any time to lose. She had suffered so many humiliations already, it didn't seem too much to ask the man who looked like a head-gardener for some advice.

'I wonder if you could tell me, do they publish any books, sort of manuals of instruction really, on how to make love . . . in an ordinary sort of way?'

'I beg your pardon?' said the gardener, and for one wild moment Julia wondered whether he in fact worked in some other shop, and she had done something unpardonable. No, of course he worked here, she had seen him directing people towards the shelves of their choice.

'Well, I was looking for something . . . to give to my niece,' she said triumphantly. 'She's . . . er, getting married soon, and I don't think she knows exactly what will be expected of her.'

The gardener looked concerned on behalf of the niece but didn't see how he could help.

'Couldn't you tell her yourself, madam?' he asked politely, but puzzled.

'Oh I have, I have,' Julia said. 'But only basic things really, and she wants to be sort of tigerish if you know what I mean. She feels she's going to lose out by not knowing the techniques that a man expects. She wants more than just clinical information, it's the response she's keen to learn really.'

'I don't expect her husband will want anybody to teach her that except himself,' said the gardener, a trifle hypocritically and pompously Julia thought. What was he doing running a porn shop, if these were his views? Oh well, I've got as far as this, she thought in despair, I might as well wade on.

'You see she's in an unfortunate position. This chap she's marrying, he's been around a lot, and my . . . niece more or less pretended that she had too, so she's going to feel very foolish when he discovers that she hasn't. I said I'd try and find a book that would tell her what to do.'

The gardener still looked mystified by it all. Oh why couldn't he understand, why couldn't he just say that there was such a book and sell it to her?

'But I don't see what she can learn from a book, madam,' he droned on, trying to be helpful. 'If I might suggest something, you'd be better off spending the money on a couple of bottles of wine, and sitting down with her and giving her the benefit of your own experience. If it's hard to talk about things like that, a drink often helps. She'd thank you much more for that than for just a book.'

Julia was now desperate, and desperate people say desperate things.

'I *can't* tell her anything,' she hissed in a low voice. 'I don't know anything. I'm a nun.'

'*A nun?*' bayed the gardener in horror.

'Well yes, we don't wear nuns' clothes these days, we work out in the world. You see, it all changed after that council in Rome, you hardly ever see nuns as nuns so to speak these days. Half the people walking around might be nuns.'

She wasn't even a Catholic, she knew only the vaguest things about nuns, but she was banking that a man who ran a porn shop might know less.

She was wrong.

'Well I never,' he said. 'My sister is a nun too. But she wears dark clothes, and a short veil like a scarf since Vatican Two.' He looked stunned at Julia's poncho cape and green trousers, at her sunglasses pushed back over the top of her scarf, and at her long, painted fingernails.

'I suppose that you Sisters must be getting more and more worldly all the time,' he said with deference.

'Well, it's so we'll look more normal at work,' Julia explained. 'Not to frighten off the other people, and make them think we are too holy or anything.'

'And do you teach, Sister, or do you work in a hospital?' he asked with awe.

'A travel agency,' said Julia before she could help herself.

'Why do nuns do that?' he asked with interest.

'It's mainly to help send people out on the Missions,' Julia replied, beginning to sweat, but thinking that in fact, it mightn't be a bad side-line for their own agency. If she ever survived this ordeal she would suggest it to the others.

'So now you see why I need that book for . . . my niece,' she went on briskly, and hoping to give the air of a worldly, business-like nun.

'Well, I really don't like to suggest anything, Sister,' he said fearfully.

'Nonsense,' Julia said. 'You must learn to accept us as we are, women working in the world, like other women. It's just that we've given up sex . . . or never taken it up,' she finished lamely.

'Perhaps a bigger store might have one of these books on preparing for marriage . . . by a woman doctor,' he said, trying to get out of it.

'I've been through those, nothing tigerish enough for my niece,' said Julia.

'Tigerish.' He thought for a while. 'We're out of tigerish books, Sister,' he said firmly.

'What would you suggest?' she begged.

'I don't think the fellow's going to mind at all, he'll like showing her around, if you'll forgive the expression.'

'But she's quite old, my niece. I mean she's in her mid-twenties, he'll expect her to know tigerish things.'

'Oh no, he won't, Sister. I'd go off and set her mind at rest about that. I mean it's not as if she was nearly thirty or something, he won't expect anything.'

Julia walked sadly out of the shop. The man who looked like a gardener rushed and opened the door for her.

'It was a pleasure to meet you, Sister,' he said. 'I hope we'll have the pleasure of seeing you here again . . . but perhaps not, of course. I'm sorry. And I'm sorry for suggesting all that stuff about the bottles of wine and the bit of chat. I mean I wasn't to know you were a nun, Sister.'

On the way back to Tottenham Court Road tube station she saw an off-licence. The gardener was probably right, maybe two bottles of wine would work better than a book. Maybe she could pretend to get drunk on Friday and see what happened, maybe she could make Michael a little bit drunk and watch what he did.

For the first time since the whole terrible problem had begun to obsess her, Julia saw a ray of hope. Perhaps it mightn't be as awful as she thought it was going to be. He was hardly going to get out of bed, put on all his clothes and say, 'You have deceived me.' It was laughable, really, and that was another thing. She and Michael did laugh together about a lot of things, they might even be able to laugh one day about the thought of a nun in cape and trousers running a travel agency for missionaries and visiting porn shops in her lunch hour.

Well, it was either believe that, or ask the good-looking Italian boy who was struggling with his map trying to find Oxford Street, whether he'd like to rent a hotel-room for the afternoon with her. And, really, Julia thought that for a twenty-nine-year-old virgin, she had coped with quite enough that day.

Holborn

Rita sat down to make a list of all the things she needed to do. Now that she had been such a fool as to agree to the whole ridiculous idea she might as well try and get through it as painlessly as possible.

She wrote LIST at the top of a piece of paper and stared at it in rage. Why had she agreed to meet them? Normally she was so quick and firm at getting out of things she didn't want to do, but his voice had disarmed her.

Ken had rung up last night and said he was in London, he and his new wife, they were still on their honeymoon, wouldn't it be nice if they and Rita and ... er ... Jeremy, was it, could get together for a civilized meal? It wasn't Jeremy, it was Jeffrey, he must have known. She knew that his wife was called Daisy, people didn't forget names, he must have done it on purpose.

She said hold a minute and she'd see if Jeffrey had planned anything. It was meant to be her excuse, she was going to come back to the phone and tell some lie.

'Right, of course,' Ken had said pleasantly. 'I hope he hasn't. It's our first time in London, and we'd love a bit of advice from a native.'

Jeffrey had said why not, it would be nice to meet them, he'd love to give them a bit of advice, he'd tell them about boat trips to Greenwich and he'd mark their card. He was full of enthusiasm. The fact that she had spent a whole year living with Ken didn't seem to disturb him in the least. What was past was past; they had both agreed that it was silly to brood.

She had come back to the phone and said it would be fine, where should they meet? Ken didn't know London at all, so he said he'd make his way to wherever she said. He wondered if they could make it straight after work or early evening anyway, because they'd want an early night.

'You haven't changed,' giggled Rita, with a small pang of jealousy that he still wanted to be between the sheets with his bird well before midnight.

'Oh, it's not that,' Ken said casually. 'It's just that we . . . well, Daisy gets tired easily. She's rather frail you know, we don't like too many late nights.'

So Daisy had turned out to be frail, had she? Marvellous, bloody marvellous, thought Rita. She was cunning to be frail, old Daisy. It meant she didn't have to go on all those wearying walks with Ken that Rita had endured, climbing hard sides of hills instead of easy ones, packing endless pairs of woollen socks for week-ends because you never knew when the next bout of walking fever would come on. How wise to be frail. Rita went back to her list-making.

Hair, she wrote. Yes, she'd take time off at lunch, an extra half an hour, and get her hair done. Silly to try a totally new style in case it didn't work, but she did need a cut and a conditioning treatment some time, so why not today? She decided that as soon as the hairdresser's opened she would ring round and get a lunch-time appointment.

She had another cup of coffee to celebrate that decision being made. Jeffrey was still asleep. Most of the world was still asleep. It was only 6 a.m., but Rita couldn't sleep.

Clothes, she wrote. They had arranged to meet at Holborn station of all places; it was the only possible meeting-point she could think of that was near Jeffrey's work, her work, and that Ken would be able to find. Ken really did sound bewildered by the size of London, not at all like the confident man she had known in Wales. Yes, clothes. She would wear her new skirt, the long patchwork one, and she would get a very simple sweater to go with it, in a matching colour, green maybe, or dark brown. She needed a new sweater anyway, it wasn't a question of buying anything specially for the occasion, that would be idiotic. What did she want to impress Ken for now? All that business was long over. She had ended it, she had left and come to London, she wasn't hoping he'd still fancy her. No, she needed a new sweater. Why not get it today? The shops in the Strand opened at nine o'clock, and she needn't be at work until half-past.

Photos, she wrote. She had a small pocket album of pictures of their wedding last year, it would be nice to show them to Ken. He would be interested, he would even recognize some of the people, her sister, her friends from Cardiff. And anyway, Rita thought, I look great in those pictures. After three months on a diet, naturally I look great. Why not let the frail Daisy have a look at me when I was two stone less than I am now? If they were still on their honeymoon, they wouldn't have wedding pictures yet, so she could be one up.

Handbag. Her own was a bit tattered, it didn't really go with the patchwork skirt, it didn't go with anything. She definitely needed one. At least twice last week she had been on the point of buying one. It had nothing to do with the fact that Daisy would probably have a frail little trousseau handbag with her either. No, she must get a handbag today.

She would borrow Lilly's cape. Lilly had a lovely black cape of fine wool with braid on the edge, which would be ideal over the outfit she was planning to wear. She must telephone Lilly at 8.30 a.m., before she left home, so that she could bring it to work with her. She had borrowed the cape twice already for parties and had lent Lilly her pendant in return. It was a gold pendant that Ken had given her. She still hadn't decided whether she would wear it tonight. Probably not.

It was still too early to talk to people, Rita grumbled to herself. She wished that people woke up sooner. Not that she could say much to Jeffrey, he would be busy getting out his guide-books to London, and his list of pubs that served Real Ale. He was so very confident of her, it would never cross his mind that she was excited about seeing Ken again, and that she was sleepless with worrying about how to present herself in a good light. Jeffrey would laugh tolerantly and say how like a woman. Jeffrey had a good comforting line in clichés when he wanted. Rita often thought he used them like warriors used armour to avoid having to meet any real thoughts head-on. Jeffrey was always pretty predictable.

Now that's one thing he wasn't. He was tiresomely unpredictable, you never knew what was going to happen. She hadn't liked it at the time and she didn't like it now, but that was the real reason she had got up so early. For all his protestations about having an early night, Ken might easily be persuaded to come back to the flat for just one drink. Jeffrey loved people to come back and so normally did she, but if Ken was going to see her home she wanted to look at it with an eagle eye herself first.

Coffee-cup in hand, Rita walked through the sitting-room. Ken would laugh at the coffee-table, not out loud but he would laugh. They used to use the word 'coffee-table' as an adjective to describe things and people they didn't like.

But what *did* you put things on, Rita complained to herself in irritation, if you didn't have a table of some sort? She just wished it didn't look so much like the kind of thing that held posh magazines and books nobody read. Well, she could cover it in things, ashtrays, knitting even. But God, how she and Ken had laughed at people who spent their time knitting. She hadn't known then that it was quite a peaceful thing to do while you watched television or listened to records. No, it might be pushing it to leave out her knitting, even though she was halfway through another great sweater for herself, and they only took her a week these days.

When she lived with Ken they had stripped down furniture and thought that the modern reproduction stuff was so ugly that it made you want to cry. She had no stripped-down pine in her sitting-room now; in fact, quite a few little desks and corner cupboards of the type they used to laugh at. Rita shook herself and reasoned that she could hardly refurnish the whole flat before 10 p.m. that night for a man who might not even see it, and for one whom she no longer loved. Yes, she knew that she didn't love him, but she wanted to think that he still loved and admired her. Having it both ways certainly, why not? A lot of people had things both ways.

Jeffrey, for example, had things both ways. He had his

freedom to go racing, she never interfered with that, and he had his home to come back to. He had her as a kind of modern practical stepmother to his two sons who came to tea every Saturday. She never bothered doing the place up for them, she never wanted to impress them with tales that they could tell their mother when they got home. Funny that she never put on any show for these two silent big-eyed children, so that they could observe and note and tell their strange, silent, big-eyed mother, Jeffrey's first and foolishly ill-considered wife.

In fact she had met Heather on a few occasions and talked to her exactly like she would have talked to a client in the beauty-salon. She regarded Heather as somebody you made conversation with, it didn't grow naturally. A lot of the women she beautified were like that, they wanted nothing about you, nothing about them, but lots of cheery stuff on the weather, the price of shoes, the traffic jams and the wisdom of taking a holiday early in the season. Rita was very good at it. Heather had been easy.

So perhaps Ken and the dreaded Daisy would be easy too. But she could never in a million years talk like that to Ken, she used to imitate salon-chat to him when they were living together, and sometimes he and she would make up a joke salon-conversation with each other ... the kind of one where both sides were eager to find some harmless incontroversial middle-ground to speak about. If Ken caught a hint of that in her conversation tonight ... an accidental little suspicion of it ... she would die. Yes, she couldn't bear him to think she had gone over to the other side, to the enemy.

It was time to ring Lilly. Lilly grumbled and said it was raining and she was going to be taking her dry-cleaning anyway, but of course agreed. 'I love a bit of excitement over people's past,' said Lilly. 'You've always been so un-eventful, happy, safe, married, never trying to pick up clients' husbands like we have. I'm glad there's a bit of drama here.'

Drama indeed! It could hardly be described as that. Much more a middle-class acquisitive wish to show off, Rita thought sadly, as she woke Jeffrey and handed him a cup of tea, because of some feeling that she was being dis-loyal to him by all this concentration on Ken. Jeffrey was pleased and touched, he looked very boyish and tousled sitting up in bed, drinking his tea as if it had been the most generous gift anyone had ever given him. Somehow this irritated Rita, and she said she was late and ran out of the flat.

She spent half an hour and almost a whole week's salary in a department store before she went into the salon. The sweater was far too dear and so were the handbag and the ear-rings that she felt she needed as well. They were all items she would have defined as luxury and out of her reach. She felt a low gloom come down on her after the initial exhilaration. A lot of eye-brow plucking, contour-massaging, skin-peeling and salon-chat went into earning that much money. She tried to tell herself that she needed a couple of nice things, but she felt guilty. The kind of people who bought handbags and sweaters at that price were usually debs or wives of tycoons. There would be problems at the end of the month when they came to do the hire-purchase repayments, but perhaps she could borrow something before then.

Lilly handed over the cape. They sympathized with each other again and again about working in the only beauty-salon in London that didn't incorporate a hairdresser's, and the day's work began. Between clients they had a giggle about how funny it would be if the dreadful Daisy came in to have a face-lift or something, and how Lilly would deliberately sabotage her.

Since she was already so much in debt Rita thought that it would be a pity to spoil the whole appearance by for-going the hairdo, so that took care of the best part of a tenner and a half-hour over her lunch-hour. The after-noon seemed very long. Lilly wanted to know all about Daisy, but Rita didn't know very much apart from her newly-discovered frailty. She had been a nurse in the hos-pital where Ken ended up after one of his falls from a cliff, and had met Ken shortly after Rita left Wales. Rita had heard surprisingly little about her from the couple of friends she still had in Cardiff. She was said to be 'very sensible' and 'very good for Ken', two remarks which Rita always assumed were in the nature of mild insults.

'Well, whatever she's like, she can't look as well as you

do tonight,' said Lilly loyally and admiringly, when the salon finally closed and Rita dressed herself up.

'I don't really care,' Rita said. 'But I'd like him to have a bit of a pang about me. It's only natural, isn't it?'

Lilly agreed it was totally the right attitude, and asked if she could sort of pass by the station too, so that she could have a look at them all meeting.

Rita didn't want that at all. It seemed too stagey. 'That's not fair,' complained Lilly. 'I've lent you my cape, I've been excited about it all day. I want to have a look. I won't say a word, I won't pretend I know you.'

'Jeffrey will recognize you,' said Rita.

'No, I'll keep my head down. Oh go on, you can't stop me anyway. It's a public street, everyone has a right to be there.'

Very reluctantly Rita agreed, and they set off about thirty yards apart from each other.

It was a mild evening, and the lights of the shops were competing with the sunset as the girls walked towards the station. On evenings like this Rita felt that she had made London her own, she lost the impersonal side of it. It was like any big town, you had your own little quarters, the place where you lived, the place where you worked, the place where you shopped. It was a matter of breaking down a huge city and making it manageable.

Lilly was ahead. She stopped to buy a newspaper, and looked up the cinema times. This was her ruse, her cover for why she was hanging about. Rita saw Jeffrey there, looking at his watch. This irritated her too, because he was early, at least five minutes early, and there he was already fussing about the time. She could see no sign of Ken and his frail bride.

Just as she reached Jeffrey, who began to make delighted sounds at the way she looked, she saw Lilly talking to a woman with a walking-stick. They seemed to be greeting each other as old friends. Rita squinted. No, she didn't know the woman, and by her appearance she was hardly a client from the salon. You had to have a certain kind of chic and a certain kind of money before you could come in and have your face slapped by Rita or Lilly. Then, with a shock that nearly knocked her down, she saw that the woman was introducing Lilly to Ken. There he was, all smiles and grins and eager handshakes, the kind of over-eagerness that meant he was shy. My God, that woman couldn't be Daisy. She was years older than everyone, she could be Ken's mother. There had to be a mistake. Daisy was around the corner, this was some dreadful old woman who knew everyone, Ken, Lilly, half of London perhaps. Wave after wave of sickness passed over Rita, she actually thought she was going to faint. Jeffrey was talking away:

'. . . really smashing, and you bought ear-rings too. They do suit you. Love, you look like a magazine cover, that's what you look like.'

'That's Ken,' Rita rapped out, pointing.

'And he's talking to Lilly,' beamed Jeffrey. 'Isn't that a coincidence?'

He started moving over in great bounds with his hand held out and Rita followed on legs that seemed too weak to carry her. She kept well away from the edge of the pavement, the slightest stumble she felt might push her out under the traffic.

'Ken!' she said. 'And Lilly! Now who says London isn't a village?'

'This is Daisy, Rita,' said Ken in the voice of a child coming home from school with his first prize.

Rita looked at her. She was forty, she couldn't have been a day less. She had stringy hair pushed behind her ears, and she lent on a stick. She had a great big smile, like someone's elderly and kindly invalid aunt.

'You're just the way I imagined,' beamed Daisy, and with her free hand clutched Rita's shoulder and gave her a sort of clumsy hug. She gave Jeffrey a hug too. Jeffrey looked as if all his birthdays had come at once. A little world of good-natured nice people had all gathered together, he was as happy as a king.

Lilly was like someone with shellshock.

'Rita told me that she was meeting friends tonight, but . . . well, isn't it absolutely extraordinary?'

'How do you know each other?' snapped Rita in a bark. She was just recovering from the hug. She hated women who embraced you, and particularly women who embraced you from the awkward position of leaning on a stick.

'Peggy's an old ... Peggy's a family friend ...' stammered Lilly.

'I used to nurse with Lilly's mother,' said Daisy. 'And when Lilly was a child I used to come to the house and scrounge Sunday lunch. Your mother was so good to us, Lilly. We young nurses never had a penny in those days and there was always a huge meal there. It was really like home.'

Ken couldn't go to bed with this woman, Ken couldn't be on honeymoon with her. She wasn't frail, she was a cripple. What had he been thinking of? He must have had some kind of nervous breakdown? Why was she called Peggy and Daisy, and why was she standing there leaning on her stick in her shabby jacket and skirt smiling all around her and looking so horribly *old*?

'Let's all go and sit down,' said Jeffrey happily. 'There's a pub near here or we can go straight to the restaurant. Lilly, you'll come with us. Shall I get a taxi?' He was so excited by it all that Rita could have hit him hard with her new handbag.

'Oh no, I can't, I have to, I mean I'm going,' said Lilly, who, to give her some credit, thought Rita, looked wretched about it all. She didn't want to come and witness the shambles of an evening that it was going to be.

'Nonsense,' said everyone at once including Rita, and suddenly there was a taxi and the five of them were in it, four of them chattering like birds in a box, Rita trying to calm down her mind which seemed to be trying to get out of her forehead.

Why had nobody mentioned to her, even in passing, that this Daisy was an old woman? Very sensible, very good for Ken, what did they mean? Ken was fifteen years younger than her, at least. That might have merited a brief remark when Daisy's name came up. Rita looked at her. She was laughing and saying how exciting it was to be in London, and that she had already seen a man who read the television news, and an actor, and thought she had seen a woman MP, but Ken said it wasn't her after all.

'Why does Lilly call you Peggy?' asked Rita suddenly.

Daisy had an explanation for that too. Daisy had been her family name, like a nickname. When she was younger and worried about what people thought of her, she thought it was a silly name to have. So in the hospital she had pretended she was called Peggy. She had two identities now, the people she knew from those four years in the training hospital, who still called her Peggy, and her real name, which she had taken up again when she got a bit of sense, and decided not to upset her parents any more than she need by rejecting the name they had given her.

They got to the restaurant. Everyone fussed about Daisy. The taximan helped her out of the cab.

'Did you have a fall, my girl?' he asked her kindly.

Girl! Rita nearly laughed aloud.

'No, it's arthritis,' said Daisy. 'It's normally not nearly as bad as this. I feel such a fool with the stick, I'm always tripping people up with it. Most of the time I don't need it at all, it's just this week it's bad. I couldn't have timed it better, a wedding and a honeymoon and a stick, wouldn't you know?' The taximan was delighted with her. So was the waiter in the restaurant. He found her a chair with arms to sit on. Quite naturally, as if she had been the one who invited them all there, Daisy started arranging where they should sit.

'Rita, sit there by Ken, you have so much to say to him after all these years, and I'll take Jeffrey and Lilly here to tell me all about London.'

There was no fuss. They were seated. Rita raised her eyes to Ken.

'It's great to see you,' she lied straight at him.

'You look lovely, like a model,' he said truthfully, straight back at her.

'I feel overdressed and stupid,' she said, with honesty and feeling.

'You were always lovely to look at,' he said. 'But I think you've got even better-looking.' His voice had a simple quality about it, like the way he used to say that mountains were beautiful, or that some piece of wood they had been scraping and stripping all week-end looked perfect. Just objective, happy admiration.

'Jeffrey's in insurance, isn't he?' said Ken after Rita had just stared at her plate for a bit.

'Oh yes, he's with a company but he does a bit of free-lancing as well.'

'Perhaps we could get a bit of advice from him. We've

got a small house. Do you remember Rodney Row? It's one of those.'

They used to laugh at Rodney Row and say they were doll's houses for doll people.

'I'm sure he'd be glad to give you any tips,' she said. 'Jeffrey loves helping people he knows, and not just to make a commission, you know.'

'Oh no I wouldn't think that, but of course we'd be very happy to do anything through him if it would help. I mean if there was any value to him out of it,' said Ken.

'I don't think he'd like to make money out of friends.'

'No, perhaps it's better not to mix work and pleasure,' said Ken agreeably, looking at the menu.

Pleasure. Pleasure. Had she remembered it all wrong? Was it she, not Ken, who was going mad? Perhaps he had always been the man who was destined to marry some age-ing nurse with a walking-stick? Those wild months of free-dom and abandon, and being sure with each other because together it was easy to reject other people's pretensions and nonsenses . . . had all that been real, or was it just in her head?

The others were laughing loudly. Daisy had said some-thing endearing to the waiter, and he had brought her a rose. She put it behind her ear, in the middle of that lank greasy hair, and smiled a big smile with a lot of yellow teeth.

'Isn't this all great, Ken?' she laughed at him down the table.

Rita wouldn't let it go, there had to be something. There must have been something there, she couldn't have got it all so wrong, her memories of what they had. If they had nothing it would be like some kind of surgery, something would have been taken out of her.

'Look at those four over there,' she said desperately indicating a table where two middle-aged couples sat eating and making occasional little forays of conversation. 'Looks like a real salon-talk set-up, don't you think?'

Oh please, please, let him fall back into it, let us both start like we did in the old days. He might say 'One thing about the Italians is they know how to cook food' and she would say 'Isn't it funny the way all Italian restaurants seem to be run by families?' and he would say 'And they

131

always seem to be so good-humoured, it must be coming from all that sun' and together they would laugh about how people could and did talk in clichés from birth to death. Please, please, let him remember salon-talk.

Ken looked obediently at the four eaters.

'They don't seem to be having a good time, is that what you mean?' he asked.

'Yes,' said Rita flatly.

'I often think that people in restaurants must look over at other tables and envy them,' he said. 'They must wish they were part of a good scene like this.' He beamed down the table at Lilly and Daisy and Jeffrey and raised his glass to his travesty of a wife, and Rita wondered with a sharp pain whether she was going to be wrong about everything else as well. Had she never got anything right?

Chancery Lane

Dear Mr Lewis,

I'm sure you will think this very, very odd and you will
spend the rest of your life refusing to talk to strange
women at parties in case something of the sort should happen again. We met very briefly at the Barry's last week.
You mentioned you were a barrister and I mentioned the
Lord knows what because I was up to my eyebrows in gin.
I was the one who was wearing a blue dress and what
started out as a feather boa, but sort of moulted during the
night. Anyway, your only mistake was to let me know
where you worked, and my mistakes that night were
legion.

I know nobody else at all in the legal world and I wonder if you could tell me where to look. In books people
open yellow pages and suddenly find exactly the right kind
of lawyer for themselves, but I've been looking in the
windows of various solicitor's offices and they don't seem
to be the kind of thing I want. They're full of files and girls
typing. You seemed to have a lot of style that night, and
you might know where to direct me.

I want to sue somebody for a breach of promise. I want
to take him for everything he's got. I want a great deal of
publicity and attention drawn to the case and photographs
of me leaving the court to appear in the newspapers. What
I would really like is to see all the letters involved published in the papers, and I want to be helped through the
crowds by policemen.

But what I don't know is how to begin. Do I serve something on him, or send him a writ or a notice to prosecute? I feel sure the whole thing will gather its own momentum once it starts. It's the beginning bit that has me worried. If you could write back as soon as possible and tell me where to start, I should be for ever grateful.

I feel it would be unprofessional to offer you a fee for this service, but since it's a matter of using your knowledge and experience for my benefit, I should be very happy to offer you some of mine in return. You may remember that I am a tap-dancing teacher (I probably gave several exhibitions to the whole room that night). So, if ever you want a lesson, I'd be delighted to give you one.

Yours sincerely,
Jilly Twilly.

Dear Tom,

Thanks belatedly for a wonderful party last week. I don't know what you put in those drinks but it took me days to get over it all. I enjoyed meeting all your friends. There was a woman with the impossible name of Jilly Twilly, I think, but perhaps I got it wrong. She wore a blue dress and a feather boa of sorts. I seem to have taken her cigarette-lighter by mistake, and I was wondering if you could let me have her address so that I could return it. She seemed a lively sort of girl, have you known her long?

Once more, thanks for a great party.

John Lewis.

Dear John,

Glad you enjoyed the party. Yes, I gather her name is Jilly Twilly, unlikely as it sounds. I don't know her at all. She came with that banker guy, who is a friend of Freddy's, so he might know. Pretty spectacular dance she did, wasn't it? The women were all a bit sour about it, but I thought she was great.

Greetings to all in chambers.

Tom.

Dear Ms Twilly,

Thank you for your letter. Unfortunately you have approached the wrong person. Barristers are in fact briefed by solicitors in cases of this kind. So what you must do if you have a legal problem is to consult your family solicitor. If his firm does not handle the kind of litigation you have in mind, perhaps he may recommend a firm who will be able to help you.

I enjoyed meeting you at the party, and do indeed remember you very well. You seemed a very cheerful and happy person, and I might point out that these breach of promise actions are rarely satisfactory. They are never pleasant things for anyone, and I cannot believe that you would actually crave the attendant publicity.

I urge you to be circumspect about this for your own sake, but please do not regard this as legal advice, which it certainly is not.

I wish you success in whatever you are about to do, but with the reservation that I think you are unwise to be about to do it at all.

Kind wishes,

John Lewis.

Dear Mr Lewis,

Thank you very much for your letter. I knew I could rely on you to help me, and despite all those stuffy phrases you used I can see you will act for me. I understand completely that you have to write things like that for your files. Now, this is the bones of the story. Charlie, who is the villain of the whole scene and probably of many other scenes as well, is a very wealthy and stuffy banker, and he asked me to marry him several times. I gave it some thought and though I knew there would be problems, I said yes. He bought me an engagement ring and we were going to get married next June.

Because you are my lawyer and can't divulge anything I tell you, I will tell you privately that I had a lot of doubts about it all. But I'm not getting any younger, I haven't been in so many shows recently, and I teach dancing when I'm not in shows. I thought it would be fairly peaceful to get married and not to worry about paying the rent and all that.

So Charlie and I made a bargain. I was to behave nicely in front of his friends, and he was to behave unstuffily in front of mine. It worked fine, a bit gruesome at some of those bank things. Merchant bankers en masse are horrific and Charlie did his best with my friends. I wasn't going to let him down in his career and he wasn't going to interfere in mine. If I got a dancing part, so long as I wasn't naked, I could take it.

And it was all fine until Tom Barry's party, and when I woke up Charlie wasn't there, he had left a note and taken my engagement ring, the rat. He said . . . oh well I'll make a photostat of the note, we'll probably need it as evidence. I'll also write out his address and you could get things going from your end.

I suppose it will be all right to pay you from the proceeds. I don't have any spare cash just now.

Warm wishes,

Jilly Twilly.

Photostat of note:

Jilly,

Now I've finally had enough. Your behaviour tonight is something that I would like obliterated from my mind. I do not want to see you again. I've kept my part of the bargain, you have failed utterly in yours.

Perhaps it is as well we discovered this before we were married. I am too angry to thank you for the undoubtedly good parts of our relationship because I cannot recall any of them.

I have reclaimed my ring. You may keep the watch.

Charles.

Dear Ms Twilly,

You have utterly misunderstood my letter. I really cannot act for you in any way in your projected action against Mr Benson. As an acquaintance, may I take the liberty of reminding you once again of how unwise you would be to start any such proceedings? You are an attractive young woman, you seem from my short meeting with you to be well able to handle a life which does not contain Mr Benson. My serious and considered advice to you, not as a lawyer but as a fellow guest at a party, is to forget it all and continue to live your own life without bitterness. And certainly without contemplating a litigation that is unlikely to bring you any satisfaction whatsoever.

Yours sincerely,

John Lewis.

Dear John,

Stop telling me what to do with my life, it *is* my life. If I want to sue I'll sue. Please have the papers ready or I will have to sue you for malpractice. You have wasted quite a lot of time already. I am enclosing a copy of the letter where Charlie mentions my marrying him. It will probably be exhibit A at the trial.

Kind wishes and hurry up,

Jilly.

Darling Jilly,

You must know that the bank can't put any money into the ridiculous venture you suggest. I didn't come to America to meet show-biz people and interest them in your little troupe of dancers. I know that it must be disheartening for you not to get any backing, but in six months' time we will be married and you won't need to bother your pretty little head or your pretty little feet about a career. I love you, Jilly, but I wish you wouldn't keep telephoning the bank here on reverse charges, because I am only here for a conference and it looks badly to get several calls a day, all about something which we haven't the slightest intention of doing.

Look after yourself if you can,

Charles.

Dear Ms Twilly,

These Chambers will have no further correspondence with you about any legal matters whatsoever. Kindly go through the correct channels, and approach a solicitor who will if necessary brief counsel for you.

Yours faithfully,
John Lewis.

Dear John,

What have I done? Why is this kind of thing always happening to me? I thought we got on so well that night at Tom Barry's party. Did I tell you by the way that Charlie was quite wrong? Tom Barry was not one of his friends, he was a mutual new friend that we had met with Freddie who was one of Charlie's friends. So I didn't break any bargain by behaving badly.

I just thought that the publicity of a big breach of promise case might give me some chance of being noticed. People would hear of me, I'd get more jobs. You see without Charlie or my ring or anything I have so little money, and I was only trying to claw at life with both hands.

It's fine for you, you are a wealthy, settled barrister. What would you do if you were a fast-fading, poor little dancer betrayed by everyone. I'm nearly 26, my best years of dancing are probably over.

It was my one chance of hitting back at life, I thought I should grab it. Anyway, I'm sorry, I seem to have upset you. Goodbye.

Jilly.

Dear Jilly,

My letter may have seemed harsh. I do indeed see what you mean about grabbing at life, and I admire your pluck, believe me I do. What you need is not so much a court action, it's much more a good friend to advise you about your career and to cheer you up. I don't think you should get involved with anyone like Charlie, your worlds are too different. I only vaguely remember him from the party at Tom Barry's but I think he was a little buttoned up.

You need somebody younger than Charlie Benson.

Perhaps you and I might meet for a meal one evening and discuss it all, totally as friends and in no way in a client–lawyer relationship. If you would like this please let me know.

Cordially,

John.

Dear Monica,

I'm afraid I won't be able to make the week-end after all. Rather an important case has come up and I can't leave London just now. I know you will be disappointed, still we did agree that I should do everything possible to advance my career, so that is what I'm doing. I hope the week-end goes awfully well, looking forward to seeing you soon.

Love,
John.

Dear John,

I was sorry about the week-end. Daddy and Mummy were sorry you were kept in London. Daddy kept saying that all work and no play ... you know the way Daddy does.

I came to London last Tuesday. You weren't in Chambers and you weren't in your flat, even though I phoned you there lots of times up to midnight. Maybe Daddy is right and although we all want to advance your career, perhaps it is a question of all work and no play.

Love anyway darling,

Monica.

Darling John,

How can I thank you for the lovely, lovely week-end. I always wanted to go to Paris and it really cheered me up. It was such a relief to be able to talk to someone so understanding. I'm afraid you must have spent a fortune but I did enjoy myself.

See you next week-end,

love Jilly.

Dear Monica,

I must say I thought your phone-call to the office today was hysterical and ill-timed. I was in consultation and it was very embarrassing to have to discuss my private life in front of others. I do not know where and why you have got this absurd notion that we had an understanding about getting married. From my side certainly we have no such thing. I always regarded you as a good friend, and will continue to do so unless prevented by another phone-call like today's.

You may check your letters from me to see whether any such 'understanding' was mentioned. I think you will find that nowhere do I mention marriage. I find this an embarrassing topic so will now close.

John.

Dear Tom,

I appreciate your intentions in writing to me with what you consider a justifiable warning. I realize you did this from no purposes of self-interest.

Still, I have to thank you for your intention and tell you

that your remarks were not well-received. Ms Twilly and I are to be married shortly, and I regard your information that she has had seven breach of promise actions settled out of court as utterly preposterous. In fact I know for a certainty that the lady is quite incapable of beginning a breach of promise action, so your friend's sources cannot be as accurate as he or you may think.

Under other circumstances I would have invited you to our wedding but, as things are, I think I can thank you for having had the party where I was fortunate enough to meet my future bride and wish you well in the future.

Sincerely,
John Lewis.

MAEVE BINCHY

VICTORIA LINE

In her journey along the Victoria line, Maeve Binchy arouses our laughter, sympathy and, as always, our delight. She allows us to eavesdrop on two former rivals plotting murder in Oxford Street, to watch a young couple travelling nervously to Seven Sisters for their first wife-swopping party and to marvel at eccentric Annie's Pimlico hotel, open only for specially chosen guests.

'Maeve Binchy has the uncluttered eye of a dramatist . . . she is a delectable stylist'

The Times

'Rare delights from an inveterate storyteller'

New Society

POST A LITTLE HAPPINESS

Post·A·Book

A Royal Mail service in association with the Book Marketing Council & The Booksellers Association.

Post-A-Book is a Post Office trademark.

MAEVE BINCHY

LIGHT A PENNY CANDLE

'The most enchanting book I have read since GONE
WITH THE WIND'

Sunday Telegraph

Compassionate, and delightful, this is the magnificent
story of twenty turbulent years in the lives of two
women. One is English, the other is Irish. Their friendship is sealed when they are children: it is warm,
devoted, unshakeable and, against all odds, it sur-
vives. Their names are Aisling and Elizabeth . . .

'Thank heavens – a thoroughly enjoyable and readable
book'

The Times

'Brilliant: a remarkable, panoramic and vastly entertaining novel'

Molly Keane, Irish Press

'A marvellous first novel which combines those rare
talents of storytelling and memorable writing'

Jeffrey Archer

CORONET BOOKS

FAY WELDON

THE PRESIDENT'S CHILD

'Delicious: effervescing and overflowing with fun'
Daily Telegraph

For seven years, Isabel Acre has guarded the secret concerning her out-of-wedlock son. She has worked at her marriage, worked at her career and forgotten the past. But the past, they say, will always catch up with you. Jason's real father is standing for the US Presidency and when the interests of powerful men coincide with those of dispensable women and children, the women had better beware . . .

The facade Isabel has so carefully maintained begins to crumble, and before long, she finds herself locked into a struggle for existence itself!

'Fay Weldon's books never fail to stir . . . she is a brilliant, needle-sharp writer'
The Bookseller

'A new and impressive debut from one of our most gifted writers'
Sunday Times

'Excellent'
London Review of Books

CORONET BOOKS

ALSO AVAILABLE FROM CORONET

MAEVE BINCHY

☐	34002 9	Victoria Line	£1.50
☐	33784 2	Light A Penny Candle	£2.50

FAY WELDON

☐	23827 5	Little Sisters	£1.75
☐	22946 2	Remember Me	£1.60
☐	25375 4	Praxis	£1.95
☐	26662 7	Puffball	£1.75
☐	27915 X	Watching Me, Watching You	£1.75
☐	27914 1	The Fat Woman's Joke	£1.50
☐	33965 9	The President's Child	£1.75

All these books are available at your local bookshop or newsagent, or can be ordered direct from the publisher. Just tick the titles you want and fill in the form below.

Prices and availability subject to change without notice.

CORONET BOOKS, P.O. Box 11, Falmouth, Cornwall.

Please send cheque or postal order, and allow the following for postage and packing:

U.K. – 50p for one book, plus 20p for the second book, and 14p for each additional book ordered up to a £1.68 maximum.

B.F.P.O. and EIRE – 50p for the first book, plus 20p for the secon book, and 14p per copy for the next 7 books, 8p per book therea

OTHER OVERSEAS CUSTOMERS – 75p for the first book, plus per copy for each additional book.

Name ....

Address ....

....